THE GIRL WHO
OWNED A CITY

THE GIRL WHO OWNED A CITY

BY O. T. NELSON

CAROLRHODA BOOKS • MINNEAPOLIS

The Girl Who Owned a City is an updated edition of a title previously published by Lerner Publishing Group, Inc. The text is completely reset in 12/15 ITC Berkeley Oldstyle Std.

Carolrhoda Books
A division of Lerner Publishing Group, Inc.
241 First Avenue North
Minneapolis, MN 55401 USA

For reading levels and more information, look up this title at www.lernerbooks.com.

The images in this book are used with the permission of: Front Cover: © Arnulf Husmo/Stone/Getty Images (burning house); © Jpaget Rfphotos/Dreamstime.com (woman); © iStockphoto.com/ Chad Thomas (grunge/orange background); © iStockphoto.com/ Cristian Dulan (grunge background).

Library of Congress Cataloging-in-Publication Data

Nelson, O. T.
    The girl who owned a city / by O. T. Nelson
        p. cm.
    Summary: When a plague sweeps over the earth killing everyone except children under twelve, ten-year-old Lisa organizes a group to rebuild a new way of life.
        ISBN 978-0-8225-3152-4 (lib. bdg. : alk. paper)
        ISBN 978-0-8225-9670-7 (pbk. : alk. paper)
        ISBN 978-1-4677-0004-7 (eBook)
    [1. Survival—Fiction. 2. Science fiction.] I. Title
    PZ7.N4358G1   1995
    [Fic]—dc20
94-29210

Manufactured in the United States of America
18 – BP – 12/1/13

FOR LISA AND TODD

PART ONE

ANIMALS, MAYBE,
AREN'T SO LUCKY.

ALL THEY DO IS WHAT THEY DO—
WHAT THEIR INSTINCTS TELL THEM.

THEY CAN'T INVENT PLANS,
AND MAKE CHOICES,
AND DREAM ABOUT TOMORROW.

CHAPTER ONE

Good! The house was empty. While Lisa waited outside in the cold to be sure, she relaxed for a moment and let herself think about the past.

At this time a few weeks ago, she had been sitting quietly in her fifth-grade social studies class. There had been no reason to believe that her life would change. Now it was the middle of December. The whole world had changed, and now life seemed terrible.

What will happen to me? she wondered. Then she swung her leg with all her might. Her boot crashed through the wooden frame and glass of the front door.

The shattering sound rang in her ears as she reached through the broken pane for the latch. Her movements were quick. She was becoming a good thief.

Her eyes struggled to adjust to the strange dimness of the room. Lucky I didn't cut myself that time, she thought, inspecting her hand. But the hand was trembling, and that made her angry.

There is nothing to be afraid of here! They're dead, and gone for good. Lisa promised herself never to be afraid again, and to prove it, she screamed at the top of her voice, "I'm here, *nobody*. I'm here!"

Not even an echo replied.

The living room was filled with expensive, comfortable furniture. The big futon seemed especially inviting and made the girl realize how tired she was.

Not thinking very clearly, she searched the room for a light switch. When she finally found one, she flipped it on. Nothing.

Dummy! she thought. There isn't any electricity anymore.

The odor of spoiled food was coming from the kitchen. The garbage container was crawling with little white maggots. They seemed to be in every kitchen, like tiny ghosts that had moved in to haunt the empty houses.

The refrigerator was filled with rotten food. She started to reach for some apples that still looked good, but she stopped, guessing that they had picked up the taste of the bad food.

She went to the pantry and loaded her sack almost to the top with canned food, mostly soup. In the bathroom, she added toothpaste, Tylenol, Kleenex, and two bars of soap.

Can opener! she remembered. She hunted around in the kitchen until she found one. Her bag was full. After grabbing some candles from the dining room table, she headed for the front door.

Her actions had become almost automatic. But she was still amazed that she could do the things she had to do—things that the world just hadn't taught her. She had heard the word "looting" before and knew that it was a kind of stealing. They had looted in the Los Angeles riots just a few years ago.

But this wasn't really looting, was it? Whoever owned this house would never be back to claim it. The food and supplies would just go to waste or be taken by some other children. Besides, the things she took would save her life—and Todd's.

Lisa moved to the light of a window to look at her watch. It was getting close to four, and Todd would be worried about her. The little brother that she used to think was a pest now depended on her for everything. She didn't mind. He had become the best thing in her strange life.

After tucking the watch into her coat pocket, she started toward the door again. She noticed a small writing desk near the window and paused. How neatly the papers were arranged on it! She couldn't resist the temptation to discover something about the people who had lived in the house. When she sat down at the desk, she suddenly felt very tired. She glanced again at the futon.

If only I were Goldilocks, she thought, laughing at herself. Then I could have a bowl of warm porridge and take a nap. But there was no time for resting.

Most of the letters on the desk were about business. As nearly as she could figure out, the Mr. Williams who had lived here had been the president of a company that made tools. There was a stack of partly addressed Christmas cards and one small, sealed letter, marked Special Delivery—Urgent. She opened it.

Mr. John Williams
Chandler Military Academy
Atlanta, Georgia

Dear Son,
I have talked seriously with Dr. Chaldon and he offers no hope to your mother and me. We are both very weak and, at the most, we have only a few more days to live. Most of the neighbors are already dead and buried. It's horrible.

On the last news broadcast, they said the virus was spreading all over the world. It's the worst plague in history.

They say that for some strange reason the sickness is not fatal to children under the age of about 12 years. No adult can survive the infection. As crazy as it sounds, soon there may be no adults left in the world, anywhere. I hope that doesn't happen.

But you, son, are too close to the "unsafe" age to take any chances. Please contact my friend Dr. Coffman in Atlanta at 456 Peachtree Street. He has promised to save you some of the new vaccine that has been working for many young people your age. Don't take any chances. Please go to see him the minute you get this letter.

I would have telephoned you, but the phone

company has gone out of business. They say that the postal system can only hold out for another 10 days. I hope they'll be able to get this letter through.

I'm sorry that we never got around to that camping trip to Canada. There are many other plans and dreams that will be lost.

Your mother and I would be happy to think that you will take this house when we're gone.

We love you, son. Be brave.

Dad

Lisa put the letter aside, recalling that she had received one very much like it. Her father had sent it from the DuPage County Hospital shortly before he died.

Tears were welling up in her eyes as she hurried away. She left the shattered front door wide open. John Williams, if he were still alive, wouldn't need a key.

CHAPTER TWO

Her house on Grand Avenue was just four blocks away. Lisa raced down Lenox toward Oak. That street was so different now. By her calculations, she had walked it more than 2,000 times, to and from school, since kindergarten. But now there was no more school, and almost every house on Oak Street and on every other street looked deserted.

No cars moved. No children played. Were there children inside those houses? It was hard to tell—everyone was hiding. It was scary.

As she rounded the corner onto Grand, she thought about the children who had disliked, sometimes even hated, their parents. Most children didn't like being told what to do or how to do it. But now all the adults were gone. Lisa was 10 years old—*she* was part of the older generation. Could she tell younger kids what to do? Or what was right and what was wrong?

Her thoughts were interrupted as she passed the second house on Grand Avenue. Jill Jansen, looking hungry, tired, and a little mean, was blocking her path. "What's in the bag?" she asked. "Can I take a look?"

After rustling through the contents, Jill demanded a few cans of soup. Ever since the plague, she had been taking in homeless and hungry children. She even had a sign in front of her house saying "Children's House," which her brother had ripped off the wall of the Montessori School.

"Jill," said Lisa, "Todd and I need all these things. I've been out searching for days, and this is the first stuff I've found." But Lisa was unable to resist Jill's plea. She handed over four cans of soup, some charcoal, and a book of matches.

Jill hadn't seen the can opener beneath the soup. That was lucky! They were valuable, and she would have wanted it. Most homes had electric openers, which were now useless. With all those kids around, the girl thought, why can't they go out and find their own food?

Todd was waiting at the door. "Lisa, I'm hungry!"

"I know, Todd, but look what I found for us—soup and matches. I was afraid we would run out. Hide the food in the space under the stairs, and give me the matches. I'll light the charcoal."

Dinner was simple—soup heated over the barbecue grill and soda crackers. They had powdered milk, mixed with water from Lake Ellyn that Lisa had boiled to make safe.

While they ate in silence, Lisa thought about their strange new life. There were no more conveniences like electric ovens or running water. No fresh milk and no eggs. No fruit, bread, butter, or ice cream. All the things that they had once taken for granted were gone. But at least they had a home, and there were empty houses where she could search for supplies.

Now Lisa was thinking of last Tuesday. Or was it Wednesday? She couldn't remember. She and Todd had gone to the Rainbow Foods at Five Corners, hoping to find supplies, but someone had thought of the idea before them. The glass door was smashed and the shelves had nothing that they wanted. The cash register had been broken open and robbed.

What will these kids do with the money? she had wondered. Money is useless now. There are no places to spend it.

She'd never forget the happy look on Todd's face when he found a kite that had fallen behind the candy counter. "Todd, you dummy! We won't have time to play with kites," she had said, and then had promised herself that they would make the time. "Oh, all right. Put it in the cart."

Lisa used to hate her little brother for getting more attention than her. But now she needed him and took care of him. It was strange how her feelings had changed. Everything was all upside down.

The shelves of that store had not been completely emptied, though. They were well stocked with all of the things that children don't like. There were cans of asparagus and spinach. She took them. The vitamin and medicine rack was still full. She emptied it. The first invaders had also left valuable stuff like candles, paper plates, and instant breakfast. She took it all.

Soon the cart was filled. Todd pushed a second empty grocery cart toward her, and they began filling it with more supplies. Lisa laughed, thinking of the stomachaches those first invaders must have had from all the candy and pop they took.

In a way, she had been glad that those things were all gone. She would have given anything for some nachos and a Coke, but she knew that Todd wouldn't eat right if their house was filled with treats.

Someone had broken a jar of popcorn, and one aisle of the store was littered with unpopped kernels. They might have been the only treat left in the world. Lisa scooped several handfuls into her coat pocket. As they left, the two children had looked back at the strange, deserted store.

"Can I have some more soup?" Todd's voice interrupted her thoughts.

"Sure. Here, Todd." She gave him what was left in her bowl and slipped back into her thoughts.

Is this Sunday? Lisa wondered, not being sure. She and Todd had to plan their days, and keeping track of the time was still important. She had given him their father's watch. When she promised to be back at a certain time, she would make sure to do so. Todd wouldn't worry if he could count the hours by his watch.

Since the plague, Todd had worked hard and learned many new things. It was one of his daily jobs to dump the garbage in the Triangle woods across the street. From Lake

17

Ellyn he carried pails of water, which they stored in the downstairs tub. Because Lisa worried about his safety, she made him carry an unloaded gun. He couldn't use it, but he could scare people with it.

Though he hated to wash dishes, he did manage to get the plates and bowls and glasses pretty clean. It was funny to watch him perch on the tall wooden stool by the sink. The dishes were going fast—he broke at least one each day. Paper plates had been nice, while they lasted.

"Hurry and get the dishes done, Todd. It's getting dark." Lisa went outside to put out the charcoal, but since the coals were still hot, she decided to make some popcorn. The sound and the smell brought back memories of picnics and family.

Other children, close by, also smelled the popping corn. Pretty soon the backyard was filled with hungry neighbors. They had spent very little time together since the plague.

The popcorn was a little burnt and chewy, but delicious. The children stood outside, while a cold wind blew through their hair and clothing. They ate in silence, washing away the salty taste with glasses of lukewarm fruit juice. They were remembering what popcorn parties used to be like.

■

Lisa had spotted the gangs roaming at night.

"Todd, bring the hammer and nails," she said. "We've got to board up the windows before we go to bed." Todd did as he was told, though he didn't understand why it was necessary.

For extra protection, they nailed several boards over each window. The job took almost an hour and, by the time they were finished, it was dark. The nails were too small, and any strong man could have ripped the boards away. But Lisa and Todd were safe tonight, because no strong man would try to break in. There were no men.

By the light of a Christmas candle, they locked the doors and went to the small room in the basement. The room had no windows and it was, they thought, a safe place to spend their nights. In the months and years before the plague, it had been used by their father as a study. The room was cold and cheerless, and they had never understood why he liked it there. But now, after many nights in that room, the two children had grown to like it. It felt safe.

They climbed into the small bed they had moved into the room. Lisa was glad to have her brother with her, and he was glad to have her, too.

"Lisa, please tell me a story," he said.

For some reason, tears started to form in her eyes and she wanted to cry. She wasn't afraid, really. Her confidence was growing. She didn't know why she felt like crying. Since that first day when they were truly alone, Lisa had been too busy for tears.

"Please tell me a story. About . . . about . . . about . . . . " He laughed because he still thought his pretended stammer was funny. She laughed too, not because she thought it was funny, but because she just wanted to laugh. He was cute when he tried to be funny.

". . . about . . . about Todd and Barney and when they went fishing," he finished.

"Well," she began her familiar story:

Todd and Barney Beagle wanted to help Lisa find food to eat. She was always bringing canned soup, and nothing was ever fresh. There was never even any hamburger. So Todd decided he would take the fishing pole out of the garage and get some worms and try to catch fish at Perry's Pond.

It was a warm, sunny day, and Todd asked Lisa to take him to the pond. He was afraid of getting lost. She walked with him and made him promise to come home in one hour. Toddy-boy looked at his watch and asked, "Would that be at ten?" She said yes and went back to the house.

Todd put his hook into the water just like Uncle Pete had shown him. Barney was wagging his tail. He liked the feel of the sun on his fur.

Nothing happened. No fish were biting. Toddy-boy wondered if there were any fish in that dumb pond. Maybe they got sick and died too, he thought.

Then he remembered that he didn't have a worm on the hook. He pulled out his line, laid it down on the bank, and thought for awhile.

He remembered that Uncle Pete used to find worms under the leaves in the wet dirt. Todd walked toward the woods and dug with his hands until he found a small worm. Barney got excited and barked at the worm.

Todd laughed at the image, and Lisa continued.

Todd went back to the place where his fishing pole was and put the worm on the hook. It looked funny hanging there, but that's the way Uncle Pete did it. Todd put the line in the water and waited.

He waited and waited, but nothing happened. He said to Barney, "We're not going to quit. We've got to catch a fish. I don't want any more soup."

They waited for a long time, and then Todd decided to move to another spot. Maybe the fish live over by that big rock, he thought, so he dropped his line in the water near the rock. He waited some more. It seemed like forever. He waited and waited until it was almost ten. I've got to catch a fish, he thought.

Suddenly, something pulled on his line. Todd pulled back. Barney stood up and barked at the strange splashing in the pond. Out came a fish. It landed on the grass and flopped all around. Barney went crazy barking at it.

Todd ran all the way home. He was proud.

Lisa cooked the fish for supper, and it was delicious. Much better than soup.

"Did you like that story, Todd?"

"Please tell another one, Lisa," he asked, in a way that answered her question.

She said, "Tomorrow night. I've got a special story about Todd and Barney and about how they solved a real mystery. But now we have to go to sleep."

The little boy did fall asleep, almost instantly. Lisa tried to sleep, but her mind was too busy thinking about tomorrow. Maybe Todd would catch a fish, but there were other important things to be done.

As Todd fell more deeply asleep, Lisa was alone once again. During the daytime, she was too busy to think or to feel lonely. But every night, in the dark and cold basement, a bad sensation came over her. She realized at these times that she was on her own.

Lisa was fearful and confused. What will become of us? was the question that seemed to pound at her in the stillness. Somehow she would have to find a way to keep them alive.

They needed food, first of all, but the supply would soon be gone. The average house contained only enough for about two weeks. By "dieting," as Lisa liked to call it, that supply might be stretched to four weeks. Those four weeks would go by all too quickly.

The stealing helped, but most of the houses and stores had already been looted. The supply of food was going fast.

Could she hunt for food? Lisa laughed at the thought of tramping through the forest with a shot-gun. It would never work. Besides, she doubted that she'd have the courage to skin a rabbit even if she was lucky enough to find and kill one.

Fishing was a good possibility. It would be easier than hunting, but there would still be the problem of cutting and cleaning the fish. She could do it, though, she decided.

After all, she'd seen her father do it often enough. She would teach Todd how to fish, and he could spend some time each day at Perry's Pond. But they couldn't depend on any one plan. She had to figure out another answer.

Could she raise food? Not until spring, and then only if she spent some time during the winter learning about gardening. There was a book about it in the study that she could read.

The thought of gardening gave Lisa a brilliant idea. Tomorrow, she would ride her bike north on Swift Road to some farms she remembered. There, she might find large quantities of food. Wow! she thought. Maybe I can find a live chicken. We can have some fresh eggs.

Now she was really getting somewhere.

Her thoughts were interrupted by the sound of scratching in the wall. It must be a mouse, Lisa decided, after hearing it a second and third time. I wonder how he survives.

Animals, she thought, were lucky in a way. They had their instincts to help them survive. It was sort of automatic, the way they knew how to find food in their surroundings. But for people, it wasn't that simple. We have to invent traps and guns and learn how to raise food. People have to think to stay alive.

Lisa had never worried about it before. Food and clothing and television and lights were always there for her use. Now everything had changed. Everything had come to a stop.

She saw the answer clearly. It was *thinking* that kept people alive and that gave them all the wonderful things.

Now that grown-ups were gone, she had to start thinking every day. Her thinking would let them keep on living.

Obviously, finding food would be a constant and frustrating problem. But at least now she had some good ideas. She could—yes, she *would*—figure something out.

Lisa glanced at the wind-up clock. It was almost ten. "I'd better go to sleep," she decided. But her mind was racing with many new ideas. Some of them made her laugh, but others were actually workable. It seemed that she had a million things to do tomorrow, and she couldn't wait to get started.

It was midnight when she next noticed the face of the clock. Lisa smiled in the dark. For the first time in a long time, she was ready for the morning.

CHAPTER THREE

Monday used to be Girl Scout day. Her old scout uniform caught Lisa's eye as she scanned her closet for something to wear. It was just a useless piece of clothing now, because Troop 719 no longer existed. The uniform still belonged to her, but she belonged to very little.

Once she had been a Girl Scout, a fifth-grader, a daughter, a ballet dancer, a friend, and so many other kinds of "belonging" that she couldn't name them all. Now she belonged only to herself and to Todd.

She tried on the uniform anyway. Somehow it made her feel good.

Anxious to start her trip to the farm, Lisa did the morning chores as fast as she could. She made the bed, wound the clocks, dressed, checked the doors and windows, and prepared breakfast in less then 20 minutes.

Todd asked his regular breakfast question: "What are

we going to do today, Lisa?"

She started to tell him that he should try fishing, but she hesitated. She had been too bossy lately. Young as he was, Todd was her partner, and Lisa knew that it would be better if they acted as a team.

A suggestion would be better than an order. "Do you think you could catch some fish at Perry's Pond?" she asked.

"Sure, Lisa." He was confident.

"Good. I'll help you get the stuff together."

"I'll find some worms," Todd volunteered, putting on his coat. "Where's the shovel?"

She helped him find it and then watched as he dragged the huge shovel toward the Triangle. She smiled, feeling certain that she would be the one finally digging up the worms.

Todd returned from the woods a few minutes later. He's given up already, thought Lisa—but she was wrong. There was a giant smile on his face and a collection of worms, twigs, and leaves in his coat pocket. They picked out the biggest worms and put them in a coffee can. After she strung the bamboo pole, Todd started out for the pond.

"Come back by ten and don't fall in the water," she said. Oops! she thought. I'm giving orders again.

"Okay, Lisa."

After he left, she eagerly set out on her own adventure. On Chidester Street she found a red, high-sided wagon. In it were a few small cars and a toy truck that she would bring home for Todd. The wagon itself would be perfect for carrying whatever she might find at the farms.

At home, she tied the wagon securely to the back of her bicycle. If she did find a chicken, she would need a cage of some kind. The wicker clothes hamper that she loaded into the wagon would work.

She would be gone for several hours, so she pocketed the last candy bar to keep the hunger away. She prepared Todd's snack—soda crackers and a packet of low-cal instant breakfast mixed with water. She hated the taste of this diet stuff, but she was very glad to have it.

Todd returned at ten without any fish. He hid his disappointment behind talk about tomorrow's fishing trip, about how he needed more time, and about how he was sure he could catch fish for them. "Fishing takes patience," he said, in a tone of voice that reminded Lisa of Uncle Pete.

"Tomorrow you'll catch some, Todd," she said. He was a good kid.

But he turned back into a sassy little brother and threw a tantrum when he learned that Lisa was going on a trip without him. "Why not?" he asked, finally, when he realized that she wasn't changing her mind.

"Because of the gangs I've been hearing at night. They are starting to steal from other families like us. Soon they'll be out in the daytime, and we have to be careful. Don't you want to be the guard of our house?"

"I guess so," he answered. He had a familiar look of worry. "How long will you be gone?"

"I should be back by three at the latest. Did you wind your watch?"

"Yes."

"Remember," she said, mounting her bike, "stay in the house, keep the doors locked, and if anyone should try to break in, hide in the crawl space under the stairs. Keep the gun with you all the time." She added, "Your breakfast is on the table."

She rode off, with the wagon clattering along behind her. On Riford Street, she saw a few faces peek from the door of a boarded-up house. She pedaled as slowly as possible, but the metal wagon still banged against the pavement, making too much noise.

A girl from Beth Bush's house recognized her and began running to meet her. For some reason, she stopped abruptly after two or three paces and then ran back inside. Lisa saw this from the corner of her eye and wondered what had stopped the girl.

Which one of my friends would be living at the Bush's house? she wondered. It looked vaguely like Becky Cliff, but it was hard to be sure. Whoever it was had not been too lucky. Her face was pale and smudged with dirt. Her hair and clothes looked neglected.

Those kids are probably wondering what I'm up to, thought Lisa. They can see that I'm off to find supplies, but they can't guess why I'm headed *away* from all the houses and stores. I hope I'm the first to think of this. I'll be mad if I pedal all the way out to these farms just to find them empty like everything else.

Lisa's leg muscles were beginning to ache, but her mind was so busy with thoughts of farms and fields that she didn't notice the pain. There just has to be lots of food there, she thought. After all, that's where food comes from.

At North Avenue, she decided to rest her legs. After pulling the bike into a deserted gas station, she sat for a while in the weak winter sun, using a gas pump for a backrest. She ate the candy bar, but it made her thirsty. A water faucet was fixed to the outside wall of the station. Perhaps there was still enough pressure in the tank to force out a little trickle of water.

To her surprise, the water came rushing out. After taking a long drink, she returned to her seat by the pump.

As she sat and stared at the big, empty road, Lisa became aware of its stillness. There was not one single car, not a sign of life anywhere.

She had made all her other visits to this intersection in the family car. Before leaving the station, they always had to wait patiently for a break in the long stream of cars. Now there was no traffic at all. The road seemed huge and strange without it.

Now's my chance to break a rule without being punished, she thought. There was no one around to tell her to look both ways before crossing the street.

She pedaled hard, held her eyes straight ahead, and crossed the intersection while looking straight ahead. She laughed out loud, and then shouted, "Many rules have become useless!" But no one heard.

Fifteen minutes later, Lisa was pedaling past farms and fields. She chose the farm that looked most inviting. It had large, freshly painted buildings and a long white fence that ran for a hundred yards or so before disappearing into a thick forest. She wheeled past the fence and parked her bike by the largest barn.

What she saw inside the barn made her feel sick. The cows had been left in their stalls with too little food. They were all dead. It was a horrible sight, and she stood for only a moment in the midst of it.

Afraid to venture into the other farm buildings, she turned her attention to the crops—but there were none. The farmer had harvested the fields long ago, and nothing remained but brown stubs and clods of dirt.

Lisa looked toward the farmhouse. The rear door was wide open, so she went inside. She could see that the house had never been looted. A few squirrels and mice had moved in, but otherwise the rooms were undisturbed.

A note lay on the kitchen table.

To the finder of this note:

We have loved this farm and our family has worked it for over forty years. Now we must give it up, and we have no children to leave it to.

Please come to live on our farm. The cows will give you fine milk. The chickens can provide eggs. If you look in the study, you will find a case of books and notes that will help you learn all you need to know about farming.

In a world without adults, you will need a simple way to live. Take this farm. It makes us happy to think that some young children will choose our place to make their new lives.

Sincerely,
Winifred Crowl

P.S. The cookie jar is filled with oatmeal and chocolate-chip cookies. The pantry has a supply of canned goods.

On the back side, in very poor handwriting, were these final words.

I think I am the last to die. I know of no other adult who is still alive. I tried to get out to feed the cattle or let them go, but I fainted and had to come back inside.

I've waited and waited. I thought you might come around while I was still alive, but now I don't think so.

While I wait, I think about you. How frightening it must be to find yourself alone in a world without the grown-ups that once made it run. There must be fear and sadness all around you. Be brave, children, be strong.

You must figure out how to make things work again—like this farm and the other things that make life so easy. You can do it. It will take time and work, but you can do it.

Another sentence was started and then crossed out. Maybe the woman didn't have the time to finish it. Or, more likely, she just couldn't dream up any good advice for the new world. She couldn't begin to imagine what that world would be like.

But she had come pretty close. With the first tears she

had shed in a long while, Lisa surrendered to the kindness in the woman's words. All this time I've been truly alone and her note . . . it's . . . it's the last I'll ever hear from those people.

She sat in silence for a long time, letting the woman's words repeat themselves in her mind. "Be brave . . . strong . . . find out how it runs . . . ." Lisa knew that she and Todd would not take over the farm. They loved their own home too much.

She brought herself back to the present. No time to waste here, she thought, shaking herself back into action. Before leaving by the back door, she used a large bag to collect flour, canned vegetables, and other supplies from the pantry.

Outside, a chicken darted around the corner of the house and hurried toward her with a haste that seemed to say, "Glad to see you!" Lisa was definitely glad to see the hen. With no effort at all, she lifted the clucking bird into the wicker basket.

The girl was swept up in a sudden mood of happiness. Although she hadn't found all that she had hoped for, the woman's note, the homemade cookies, and the live hen encouraged her. If only her wagon were a little bigger . . .

The good mood brought a reckless idea to her. It was an idea that made her laugh a bold, confident laugh. Instead of making endless supply trips with the bike and wagon, she would learn to drive the car. Today!

Her father's words ran through her mind. "Stick the

key in the ignition, turn the key, put it into Drive, and go." He had said them so many times to her mother, sometimes apologizing for his bossiness. But Lisa was happy that she remembered his repetitious directions. They would give her enough to go on. She would soon remember the others, and she would be driving! Lisa couldn't wait to see the bewildered look on the faces of the Riford Street kids when she made her first trip in a car.

She barely noticed the passing scenery on her bike ride home. She was thinking about the car ride. She could do it! As she passed North Avenue, the gas station, and the blank, peering faces on Riford Street, she rehearsed the details of her plan. Her father's instructions came to her clearly now, as if they had been stored on tape somewhere in her brain, waiting to be called into use. "Keep it in park till you're ready to go . . . let it warm up a minute . . . look around you . . . keep your foot on the brake . . . put the shift lever in Drive . . . let up on the brake . . . not too much gas . . . slowly now . . ."

The driveway of her house appeared. Quickly, she pulled the wagon and bike into the garage. The sight of the big car made her stomach feel funny. "I'll never—" she started to say, but stopped, knowing that she *must* try it. She emptied the wagon and called out to Todd to tell him her plans.

"Really?" Todd was excited. "Let's go now!"

"I didn't say *we*, Todd. I have to try this alone." But it was too late to avoid his outburst. She wished that she had used a different way to tell him.

Finally he stopped arguing, and they made peace. "It's dangerous, and I have to learn how to drive first," she explained. "You can go some other time."

Lisa drew a map of her course and traced the route to North Avenue with her finger. "If I'm not back by three-thirty, come looking for me."

He watched her climb into the car. "Be careful, Lisa." His warning surprised her. Was he imagining his own fate if something actually did go wrong?

She sat behind the wheel and struggled to adjust the thick, cushioned seat. The dashboard seemed to loom above her, and her feet barely touched the pedals. Lisa was frightened. Ten-year-old girls just didn't drive cars. What made her think that *she* could?

Her body shook in silence for a long time. "Damn tears!" she said out loud. Then she laughed at her first real swear word. Somehow it made her feel better. Wiping the blur from her eyes, she said it again, louder this time.

They needed those supplies, and getting them would take 10 trips with the wagon. Besides, someone else might find the stuff before she could get it all moved. If she could learn to drive this car, then she and Todd could really stock up. That would give them time to make better plans.

The future had not been very clear, but now she could imagine months and years of finding food and trying to survive. The car would help a lot. She looked at the fuel gauge—full. Good thing the car is facing out to the street, she thought. I'd never be able to back it out.

She remembered the instructions again. "Turn the key . . ." The engine came alive with a powerful roar. As if frightened by the sound, her foot jumped away from the pedal. The roar became a soft whir.

"Look all around you." As Lisa recalled the command, her eyes traced a circle around the car and passed a pale boy—her brother—framed by the garage door.

"Keep your foot on the brake . . . put the shift lever in Drive . . . let up on the brake . . ." The car crept forward.

"Here I go." The words stuck in her throat. Slowly, she reminded herself.

It seemed that she was flying to the end of the driveway. She turned the wheel a little too sharply and began driving across the Coles' lawn. There was a crunching sound, and then Lisa saw a clump of broken plastic where Mr. Cole's Rollerblades had been lying in the grass. If he were still alive, he would have been angry.

"Not too much gas . . . slowly . . . ." Her foot hadn't touched the gas pedal, yet she was still moving. Why am I moving? Is something wrong? In a panic, she stepped down hard on the brake. The car screeched to a stop as her head banged against the steering wheel. It was too late to recall her father's words: "Easy on the brakes!" Lisa was stunned.

In a few moments her head cleared, but it still ached above her right eye. Dummy, she thought. Easy on the brakes! She wouldn't make that mistake again.

The nervousness began to leave her. She eased up

on the brake and set off very slowly, aware of the many astonished eyes that were following her.

Her whole body was working to control the car. She felt as though she had become a part of the machine. "Don't you worry, Toddy-boy," she muttered. "I'll be back soon."

For weeks, Lisa had longed for the sight and sound of a moving automobile. A passing car would have meant that not all the adults were gone, and that the nightmare wasn't true. Now she was thankful that there was no traffic. It made her task much easier.

Slowly she guided the car toward the farm. Down Riford, to St. Charles, to Swift Road, across North Avenue. On the straight stretches of road, she practiced moving the brake and gas pedals. Her top speed of 10 miles per hour seemed like 100.

At the farm, she loaded the car all the way to the ceiling and then cautiously inched her way back toward home. As she pulled into the driveway, Lisa was deep in thought. It would have taken at least six full days with the wagon to get this much stuff. If she didn't waste gas, this car could save their lives. She had never thought about a car that way before.

Proudly, she honked the horn. Todd ran out to meet her, and together they unloaded the supplies. When the car was empty, she said, "Todd, it's only three and I have time for another trip. Carry all this stuff in-to the house. Put all the canned things in the hiding place under the stairs. If you run out of room, use the freezer. It will be a good storage space that we can lock. If there still isn't enough room in the freezer, use the washer and dryer."

"Why the washer and dryer?" Todd asked.

"The gangs probably won't look there if they break in. You can put all the tools and other stuff that isn't food in the furnace. Just slide up the furnace door."

He stared at the huge pile of food. "Okay, Lisa, but hurry back. I'm hungry."

She pulled some cookies from her pocket, then said, "I've got a surprise treat for you tonight. You'll like it." By the time she had the car started again, the cookies were gone.

As she drove away, some new, hidden eyes followed her. Their expression was not astonishment. It was something quite different.

I should have been more careful, thought Lisa. Maybe a gang saw the load I brought home. It was dumb to honk the horn and then leave Todd unprotected with all that stuff in the driveway. But she couldn't turn back—she still had time for one more load.

After reaching the farm and loading the car once again, Lisa hurried back. Already the driveway was empty. The little rascal must have run up the stairs with every load. She happily promised herself to tell him two stories that night.

Realizing all that she had to get done before dark, Lisa rushed to unload the supplies into the garage. They could hide them later if necessary. Tired, she rested a moment against the car before making an-other trip to the garage. "What a magnificent thing, that car—"

Suddenly a rock smashed into the rear windshield.

Then Lisa heard a laugh from the Triangle woods. In an instant, it all became clear. "Todd!" she cried, as she ran into the house. Where was he? She searched the rooms. He was gone. "Todd! Todd!" No answer.

He was nowhere to be seen. The upstairs was silent, empty. As she walked past the hiding place she heard a muffled, frightened sob. She knew where he was. The light from the open doorway fell upon his face. He was bleeding.

"Oh, Todd . . . oh, Todd." He looked at her and clung to her. For a long time, she couldn't speak.

Finally she asked, "What happened?"

"I . . . I . . . was bringing things into the house when they came. They took our food. They were mean to me, Lisa."

"Don't worry, Todd. I won't let it happen again. Who were they?"

"I don't know. They pushed me and hit me and said we couldn't have that stuff." He stopped crying.

She studied his injuries—a bloody lip and some minor bruises. She dried his tears and blotted the blood from his lip with a towel. "Rest here on the couch, and I'll make a supper."

He was pleased when she served the Spam and noodles, and his fright disappeared altogether when she offered him a candy bar for dessert.

The gang had only taken what was in the driveway. So the chicken was gone. But they hadn't bothered to look in the house. Perhaps she had interrupted them, though she couldn't imagine why they would be afraid of *her*.

Before securing the house that evening, Lisa locked the car and hid the key. Later, in their small room, she stared into the candle flame. She was too tired to blow it out and too excited for sleep, so she thought about the day that had just passed. It seemed that things were beginning to take shape, but she wasn't happy about what had happened to Todd.

First thing tomorrow, she had to find new hiding places for the supplies. The house also needed some defenses. Her thoughts drifted back to their bed, and she became aware, without looking, that Todd was wide awake and thinking, too.

"Hey, Todd." Her voice was loud in the silence of the study. "What are you thinking about?"

He avoided her question with one of his own. "Will you tell me a story?"

"Sure." Lisa thought for a long time and then began.

There was a boy about your age, Todd, who lived many years ago. He and his older sister were living in a poor old house, alone, because their parents were gone, just like ours. The other people of the town were very poor, and they didn't have much time to help the two orphans out, so the boy and girl had to take care of themselves.

The town hadn't always been poor. There used to be a big factory where the men and women worked. But the owner of the factory died, and no one wanted to keep it going anymore. Many people moved away, but a few families stayed. They got poorer and poorer, but they stayed.

The father of the boy and girl had held a good job in the factory. It was his work to design the candles. For many years, candles that he designed were sold all over the world. Some were plain, and others came in beautiful shapes and colors. Christmas was the best time of year for the town because the factory sold thousands of Christmas candles.

After the father died suddenly, their mother kept the children alive by raising chickens and vegetables. But one day, she became sick. Her illness lasted a long time, and she had to stay in bed. So she taught the boy and girl how to care for the chickens and how to tend the garden. Each morning they would take eggs and vegetables to the highway and sell them to the passersby. Their store was a large table with a sign that the girl had made.

Even after their mother died, the children kept selling chickens and vegetables on the highway. They earned very little, but it was enough to buy more food. There was no school, but they kept busy. In fact, their life was sort of like ours is now.

One day, while the girl was at the stand, some boys came to steal their chickens. They were mean to the little boy and hit him. He was afraid, and sad too, because he couldn't stop them. He knew that the chickens were very important.

When the girl came home and found what had happened, she cried a lot. Then the little boy started crying, because if his sister cried, it must be very bad. She hardly ever cried.

The little boy went to bed and thought about what would become of them. He thought he was no good to anyone, and he said to himself over and over again, "You couldn't fight those boys or even save the chickens." He thought, sadly, that there wasn't time for him to grow up to be helpful, because they would starve first. He felt like a coward.

But he knew that feeling sorry for himself was a waste of time. Suddenly, he had an idea that stopped all of his sad thoughts. He knew what had to be done and that he could help.

He woke his sister and proudly told her his plan. "When the candle factory was still working, everything was okay. But after the factory stopped, everyone became poor like us. So let's open the candle factory!"

His sister didn't say a word. He thought that she didn't like his idea, but he continued, "We can make candles just like father used to for Christmas presents. It's easy, and people like candles!" He was excited.

Still his sister said nothing. He was sure his idea would work, and all his cowardly thoughts seemed gone forever. "It will work! Don't you think it will work?" he asked.

"Yes," said his sister, "I think you're right. Christmas is coming and people will buy candles. The factory is still sitting here. Maybe we can talk to some of the townspeople to see if they want to open the factory again."

The little boy went to sleep, feeling very happy and proud.

The next day, the two children went to see every family in the town. But nobody wanted to help. Many said, "We don't know how to run a candle factory." Some said they were too busy. Others laughed at the boy, making jokes about the "little businessman."

He didn't care. He was sure his idea would work, so he went with his sister to the candle factory to look around. They found that all the candle-making machines had been taken away. The only thing remaining was a supply of wax. But it would be enough to start with.

They used what was left of their money to buy more wax and coloring and made their candles by hand. They heated the wax over the stove and mixed in the color. Before the wax cooled, they poured it into different sizes of cans that held string down the middle for the wicks. As the days went by, their candles got better and better. They were too busy to wonder if they would succeed.

The girl made a huge sign that said "Christmas Candles—Two Dollars." On Saturday, they both went to the highway. It was one week before Christmas.

Many people stopped to admire their handiwork. By noon, they had sold all their candles and had earned $200. They were so happy and excited that they ran all the way back to the factory to make *more. By Christmas Eve, they had made over $500. They were the happiest children in the world.*

At home that night, the girl said, "I have a surprise. Wait in the other room till I call for you."

It seemed like forever, but the boy waited patiently. Finally she called him into the room.

There on the table were three packages, wrapped in Christmas paper. "Merry Christmas!" she said.

Excited, he opened them and found a book, a shiny toy car, and a box of his favorite candy. They were his first presents in three years. He kissed his sister, saying, "But I don't have a present for you. I'm sorry."

"You gave me a wonderful present," she replied. "Your idea saved us." They made plans to really start up the factory again and go to school and many other things.

They talked a long time before the girl blew out their candle. It was the first one they had made.

"Did you like that story, Todd?"

He said that he wanted another. Lisa told him another—this time a short one. When that story was finished, his mood began to change. He lost his self-doubt—he was no longer a cowardly little kid.

He soon fell asleep. Everything was quiet, except for the sound of soft breathing. In the darkness, their problems seemed easier.

She could see now what they had to do. They must hide their supplies—in the walls, in the furniture, under the floor, in the furnace, and in places that would protect them from any invader.

Next, she had to figure out a means of defense, and she knew it wouldn't be easy. Perhaps booby traps in the yard would work. Even better, they could string a fine thread around the house that would trigger an alarm and start an avalanche of rocks falling from the roof. That's it! she thought. Above the front and rear doors . . . and then some new weapons . . . the gun wouldn't be enough.

Once their defenses were in place, she could make more trips to the farm. But she had a feeling that the farm's supply wouldn't be nearly enough. Soon the other children would think of the farm, and then what would she do? Where would she go for food?

She thought and thought, and her thoughts turned to dreams about a fantastic place with rows and rows of her favorite foods, stacked against the walls and as high as the ceiling.

Sometime in the night, she awoke. She was thinking of the words *warehouse . . . warehouse . . . a place where things are stored*. How had that come to her? She lit the candle, climbed out of bed, and began thumbing through the telephone book. Finally she found what she wanted: *Groceries—Wholesale*.

Here it is, a Jewel Grocery Warehouse on North Avenue. Close enough, she thought. And I'll bet no one else has even thought of it! Her mind wandered through the fabulous place for a long time, conjuring scenes of the endless supply of food she might find. She had to go there soon.

But she couldn't leave Todd alone again, at least not until a better defense plan had been arranged. She would call a meeting of the kids on Grand Avenue to form some kind of militia. By cooperating, they could protect one another from the gangs. If they planned together, they could even figure out a way to survive after the new supplies were gone.

Her thoughts went on and on until they became dreams again. Her parents wouldn't have believed it. They had known that Lisa was smart, but would they have believed that she could survive so cleverly? That she could drive a car or provide for a family?

Everything had changed, and Lisa wasn't really 10 years old anymore. She may have earned good marks in math and English, but now she was struggling to pass a frightening course in survival. The old life had disappeared, and had left many clues. Somehow, she would survive, and succeed.

CHAPTER FOUR

Todd awoke, crying, just before dawn. Probably a bad dream, Lisa thought. And no wonder, considering all that's happened.

By the time he was asleep again, Lisa was wide awake. She felt that it must be light outside, and her clock confirmed it. It was seven. Quietly, she dressed and slipped upstairs from the basement.

Outside, the morning sun warmed her as she studied their house on the hill. It would be easy, she decided, to defend it from the hungry and frightened children in the neighborhood. But she just couldn't believe that it was necessary. Couldn't they find a better way?

Lisa's attention turned to the car. Teaching herself to drive had been a brilliant idea, and she didn't mind giving herself a compliment. Yes, brilliant—almost like inventing something. The car had been useless before, and now it was a treasure.

But . . . the tires! Terror swept through her when she saw that the tires were flat. Why? She fell to her knees and studied the rubber with her hands. Had they been cut? No, she could find no cuts or holes.

A thing like this couldn't just happen. Who would have done it? And why? What could they gain by it? Did they want to beat her to the supplies? Were they jealous? She had brought the car back to life and used it to find food. Now someone had simply and horribly destroyed it. There was no good explanation. It was evil.

Her mind was filled with so many questions that she barely heard the voice that was calling out from the house. "Lisa, I'm hungry."

"Oh, Todd!" she cried. "They've ruined our car. Look at the tires!"

He walked to the car and, with a calmness and confidence that she hadn't seen in him before, examined the tires. Without speaking, he walked into the garage and returned with the tire pump. "Here," was all he said.

They fumbled for a time before they were able to attach the hose to the tire. They began pumping the air. It was very hard work, but before long, the car stood as high as it had before.

"Todd, you're a genius!" Her words brought a wide grin to his face that stayed all through breakfast.

"I'll do the dishes this morning," she said, wanting to reward him, "if you'll start collecting some things for me. Today we're going to fix this house up so that all the gangs in Glen Ellyn together won't be able to get in."

In response to Lisa's commands from the kitchen, Todd worked quickly to gather their supplies—hammer, saw, thread, rope, tin cans, cardboard, razor blades, and crayons.

The first project of the day would be the alarm system. Lisa explained that it was logical to start that way, because the alarm could warn them of trouble even as they worked. "Get the thread, Todd. I'll get some coat hangers."

He was puzzled and asked, "What is 'logical?'" The new word interested him. After all, as "captain of defense" he should know such grown-up words.

"I'm not sure how to explain it," she answered. "Lots of times, when you read a word in a book, or hear it said together with other words, it makes sense, even though you don't know what it means, exactly. It seems to fit, but you can't explain it. I think that logical means . . . ." She paused to ask him for the hammer, which she used to pound a nail into their fence.

"I think that logical means that things fit together right. Like in a puzzle, when a piece fits in only one way, or like . . . ." She searched for a better example while tying the end of a thread around the nail.

"Things work in a certain way. If you do things right, it's logical. When the tires were flat, I just stared at them and, of course, that didn't help. Doing that wasn't any more logical than crying or kicking the car. But you got the tire pump because you knew they needed air. *That* was logical!"

That satisfied him. He nodded to show he understood and then turned to their work.

Without much more conversation, they proceeded with the alarm system. From the nail on the fence, Lisa strung a black thread around the house on short stakes made from coat hangers. Anyone approaching their house would catch the thread just below the knees.

Next, on each side of the house, they ran threads through small holes in the window glass. Inside, they hung a rock over a carefully arranged stack of cans on each window sill. If an intruder broke through the thread, the rock would fall and topple the cans. The sound of clattering aluminum cans would be their alarm.

They were both clumsy with the tools, and it took several hours to complete the job. Lisa spent most of the time just thinking about what to do next.

When the alarm was finished, they stood on the sidewalk to make an inspection. "Good work, Toddy-boy," she said. "You can't see a thing—the thread is almost invisible. Now let's see if it works. Go inside and stand by the living room window and listen. But don't touch anything. And Todd," she called after him, "watch out for—" It was too late.

Running toward the house, eager to watch his creation work, Todd caught his legs on the thread. It broke and set off a loud clatter in the living room. Sheepishly, he turned to Lisa and surprised her by shouting, "That was not logical!"

Lisa laughed. Either I'm a good teacher, or he's a smart student, she thought. "But our alarm is logical," she called back. "It works! I could even hear it from the sidewalk!"

They reset the front alarm and repeated the test on the other three sides of the house. After some minor adjustments in the back, the alarm system was finished.

During lunch, Lisa briefed him on the afternoon's work. First, they would make warning signs reading: PRIVATE PROPERTY, DO NOT GO BEYOND THE SIDEWALK. TRESPASSERS WILL BE SHOT. Next, they would make secret storage places inside the house. Todd listened carefully as she described a series of booby traps that they would make.

"The alarm system and the other things will be your responsibility, Toddy-boy. You'll have to check them every day to make sure they're working." Her words made him feel important.

They set to work and, by four, most of the plan had been accomplished. On the roof in front and back they had rigged large boards that held back rocks and glass bottles. If an enemy approached, Todd would pull a wire to release the boards, causing an avalanche of stone and glass to roll down on the invaders.

For good measure, Lisa added a small note to the bottom of each warning sign:

P.S. If you are not friends with our German shepherd, Hans, please wait here so we can put him inside.

She thought it was a good finishing touch. They put away the tools and went into the house to write the invitations for the meeting.

Her message was simple. She wanted to create a neighborhood militia for protection against the gangs. She hoped that the neighborhood children would attend the meeting and bring their ideas. The meeting would be held in the street in front of their house at two in the afternoon on Friday. In the invitation, Lisa also promised special refreshments.

As Lisa approached Julie's house to deliver the first invitation, she felt a new sense of excitement, almost as if she were going to meet a new friend. Since the day that Lisa had moved to Grand Avenue, six years before, they hadn't spoken or played together much. True, they had argued about a few things. But now they were both just trying to survive.

It was Charlie, not Julie, who answered the door. "What do you want, Lisa?" His tone was rude.

"I want to talk to Julie," she said, wondering what his problem was. Maybe being the new man of the house had gone to his 10-year-old head. Or, she thought, maybe life with Julie and his other sister was getting to be too much for him. That possibility made her smile.

"What's so funny?" he demanded.

Forcing the smile away, she replied, "Nothing, Charlie. Will you call Julie? Please."

"She's sick. You can go up to her room." He let her in.

The house smelled awful and looked even worse. Danny, their English setter, had been living inside with them, and no one was bothering to clean up his messes. In fact, no one had cleaned up anything. The kitchen was full of dirty dishes and creepy little black bugs.

Lisa picked her way through the clutter and entered Julie's room. Julie was lying in her bed, eyes open, doing nothing. Several books were by her side and scattered across the floor.

"Hi, Julie. What's the matter?"

"Oh—hi, Lisa, I just feel kinda crummy. When I stand up sometimes I get dizzy. I don't know what it is." Her voice was very soft.

Trying to be helpful, Lisa said, "Scott Kopel used to get dizzy like that. He took vitamins because his doctor said his diet wasn't right. You should take vitamins."

Julie glared. It was the same old silly argument they used to have. "Lisa, your family is goofy about pills. Vitamins are a waste of time."

"I know, Julie, that's what your mother used to tell you. But that was when she was here to feed you decent meals. What do you eat now? I think you should—"

The sight of Julie's tears stopped the argument. Lisa recalled her own words and guessed that the word "mother" had started the crying.

"I'm sorry, Julie. I was just trying to help."

But Lisa had guessed wrong. It was the talk about food that had made her cry. Julie explained in rapid, nervous words that they were actually starving. Lisa guessed that this also explained Charlie's bad mood.

"Charlie has been out every day, but he can't seem to find any food. We've been eating Halloween candy and crackers for five days." With a tiny bit of a smile, she added, "I never thought I'd say it, but I hate candy."

"Why didn't you ask me for help, Julie? I would have

helped you. I *will* help you. I'll be right back. Want some soup? I don't have your favorite chicken noodle, but—" Lisa started toward the door.

"Wait a minute, Lisa. There's something I have to tell you first." Julie seemed nervous. She paused a while before continuing.

"The reason we didn't come to you was, well, ah, you see . . ." She stopped again.

"What is it, Julie? What's wrong?"

"Well," Julie went on, forcing out the words, "we couldn't ask *you* for help. How could we? After steal-ing from you? Lisa, I'm sorry. I couldn't stop them."

Lisa was stunned. She felt like slapping her sick friend. In disbelief she asked, "Do you mean that *you* were there yesterday with the gang that stole our supplies and beat up Todd?" It couldn't be true.

"Not exactly. I was here in bed, but I knew about it and I suppose I could have stopped them, but I didn't. So I'm guilty, and I'm truly sorry, Lisa. Will you forgive me?"

Lisa couldn't answer. Instead she asked, "How did you know about it?"

"The Chidester Gang was in the Triangle yesterday watching you make your trips for food. Tom Logan came to the door to ask Charlie to help steal the things in your driveway. Charlie wanted to join the gang because he didn't think there was anything else he could do. He didn't want to steal from *you*, Lisa. But Tom told him he had no choice. Either he helped them, or he would never get into the gang. So he helped, and I knew about it. I'm sorry."

Lisa knew that Julie meant it. "Julie," she said, "whatever you do, don't let Charlie stay with that gang. Nothing gets so bad that you have to start doing wrong things. There are better ways—ways that won't hurt anyone.

"Now, I'll get the soup while you talk to Charlie," Lisa added. "By the way, why don't you have food if Charlie helped them steal all of my stuff yesterday?"

"It's a rule of the gang," Julie answered. "New members don't share until they've been on three raids. Charlie is supposed to meet them tonight at eight for his second raid."

Lisa left the room and passed Charlie on her way out. "Your sister wants to talk to you . . . now!" she told him angrily.

Julie and Charlie were still shouting in the upstairs room when Lisa returned with a bag of food. They must have had a real argument, thought Lisa. But the shouting stopped as soon as she slammed the front door.

The moment Lisa entered Julie's room, Charlie began to argue in his own defense. "We need food, and I can't find any by myself. I've looked for days. There just isn't any. The gang promised me that we would have food if I joined in. I didn't have a choice."

"No choice, Charlie?" Lisa challenged him. "No choice but to steal from Todd and me so you can eat? Do you think I believe that?" She began walking toward him.

"Maybe if you spent less time feeling sorry for yourself, you could figure out something better. Right this minute I can give you a dozen ideas about how you can eat till you get old and fat, and none of them include stealing. But I'm not helping anyone who wants to live by stealing from me."

"But, Lisa," he pleaded, "we were scared. We thought we would die. Julie was sick, and there was no food and no one to take care of us. We're still scared. We're starving! It's my job to keep us alive and I'll do anything I—"

"Anything?" Lisa stopped him. "Even if it means hurting others? Listen, Charlie, nothing makes that okay. I don't care how scared you are."

Lisa's angry words surprised even her. It wasn't that these ideas were new to her. She had heard them from her parents in many ways before. But now she could really understand why the ideas were so important. She and Todd were working hard and felt proud to live by their own efforts. When someone thought that hunger gave them the right to steal—now *that* made her mad.

"I'm not going to join the gang, Lisa," Charlie promised.

"Sorry, but I don't trust you. And I won't give you much help. Not yet, at least. If you want some advice, here it is. There *are* places where you can find supplies. Take my word for it. Spend some time tonight thinking, instead of feeling sorry for yourself, and see if you can figure out where those supplies are. And if you don't want to be afraid anymore, then come to the meeting Friday and we'll make plans that will help us all." Lisa handed him the notice.

"In other words, Charlie, use your head. Just think, and you can take good care of your family." She was finished.

Julie had not spoken. She had been listening in amazement to Lisa talk like some grown-up. How could Lisa have changed so fast?

"Charlie, there's a bag of food downstairs by the door," Lisa said, not looking at him. "I brought it because Julie is my friend." Then she left.

At the Coles' house, on the other side of her own, Lisa found a similar situation. Cheryl was 11; her brother Steve was 12. The rest of the family was dead. Now Cheryl and Steve were running out of food and, in desperation, Steve was also planning to join the Chidester Gang. Lisa urged him to wait until after the meeting but spared him the lecture she had given Charlie.

Craig Bergman was the oldest kid on the block. At 12, he was just young enough to miss the sickness. He and his six-year-old sister, Erika, lived in the corner house, at Chidester and Grand. They had a good supply of food and were doing a little better than the other children. Craig knew a lot about gardening, and he told Lisa of his plans for the spring. Until then, he admitted, they would have a hard time.

Jill Jansen's house had at least eight orphaned children in addition to her younger sisters, Katy and Missy. Most of the children were under five. Jill was 11.

Before leaving the Jansens' house, Lisa made the same request she had made of the others. "Please think about some kind of neighborhood defense. We have to find a way to protect ourselves from the gangs. Bring some ideas, and be sure to have everyone in your house come along."

That night the candle was out, but the wax was still warm, when Todd asked for his story. It was too late—the storyteller had fallen asleep.

CHAPTER FIVE

The days before Friday were filled with hurried activity. From daylight to dusk, Lisa and Todd struggled to get more food and to keep it safe. There was never enough time.

The short winter days were cloudy, gray, and depressing. Lisa was sure that everything would get easier as the days got longer. The thought of spring warmed her inside.

Despite her problems, Lisa never got tired of "figuring things out." With each new crisis, a solution seemed easier than before. She liked the new feeling of confidence, even though it surprised her.

Lisa's thoughts were focused on the meeting. What could they accomplish? Would the kids on the block agree to a militia? She had visions of earlier days, when she had formed clubs with her friends. They were really a joke compared to this. She had to plan for this meeting and make it worthwhile.

Lisa decided to cancel her supply trips for that day and study for the meeting. She pulled out a notebook from her social studies class. There were doodles all over the cover and a lot of drawings on the inside. But there were notes inside the book, too. Perhaps there was an idea in there.

After putting the notebook away, she began planning a kind of "government" for Grand Avenue. She would make it independent, like those presidents had done for the United States centuries ago.

She thought about the Pilgrims at Plymouth Rock, who had faced the same problems she was facing. They had worked long days hunting and building their farms so they would have food. They had no interactive TV, no racks of compact discs and CD-ROMs, no video games, electricity, microwaves, or grocery stores. They had to fight Indians and somehow survive months of winter with little food. It all seemed a lot worse than dealing with the childish threats of Tom Logan and his gang.

Comparing her life to that of the Pilgrims made Lisa feel better. "What am I complaining about?" she thought. "At least I have a house, and canned food, and all of the things that the adults left us."

But she was getting ahead of herself. First, she and the other children had to solve the problem of survival. They needed to plan for food and for their own defense. They needed a militia, as the colonists had called it. A militia would be the first order of business.

She also had to get everybody planning for spring gardening. She would share her ideas about the farms and the warehouses. But they must promise her a militia first. If they could join together for defense, they would be able to plan beyond food for the next day.

But what if they wouldn't agree to a militia? What if they couldn't see how important it was? What if they were so worried about food that they promised to start a militia and then didn't go through with it? Well, she had to take that chance.

Then she had an idea—a strategy for the meeting. She would bargain, make an offer. In the end there would be a neighborhood militia to protect "individual rights" on Grand Avenue—though she didn't fully understand, yet, why individual rights were so important.

She pondered it and rehearsed it as the kernels hissed and popped in the fire. When the last batch of popcorn was made, Lisa was ready for the meeting.

Todd was carrying a giant bowl of popcorn and a pitcher of juice. Lisa brought the paper cups and a large canvas bag tied at the top. They saw children leaving their houses and gathering in the street.

From the beginning, Lisa knew that this would be different from the old club meetings. There would be no laughing or giggling. They were just as serious as the Pilgrims must have been. These children seemed to know already that their lives were at stake.

A restless, eager line formed for a share of popcorn.

Julie and Charlie were there. The Coles had shown up, and so had Craig Bergman. When the food and juice were gone, Lisa sensed that her audience was ready. She began.

"Yesterday Todd was beaten up, and we were robbed by the Chidester Gang. Tonight you too may be beaten up and robbed.

"I called this meeting because I think we need to figure out a plan to protect ourselves." She paused to let the message sink in, and then she continued. "I think we need to have a volunteer army to protect our freedom. The Pilgrims called it a militia. If we each have a signal, like a dinner bell, to warn us that someone is being attacked, then we can all join together and scare off the gang. One person could stay in each house to guard it, but all the others would come to help the family being attacked. Every house would have a different alarm so we would know where to go.

"For our house, Todd can blow a blast on his trumpet. You could each figure out a loud signal of your own. One person could volunteer to be in charge of organizing the weapons and making defense plans. Probably an older boy, like Steve Cole, could work out the details and be our general.

"That's my suggestion. Do you have any comments?"

The children could hardly recognize the new Lisa. She still *looked* the same, with her straight blond hair and deep-set eyes. But there was something different in her voice, something strong and confident. They wondered about it. For a while, everyone was silent.

Then Craig said, "I think you're excited over nothing, Lisa. Has anyone else been bothered by the gangs?"

No answer.

Lisa wanted to reply, but she thought, No, let them argue it out a while. Then it will be my turn again.

Charlie said, "I think we should form a gang of our own. None of us has food, and there won't be any unless we steal it. We're dumb not to make a strong gang ourselves. If we wait, the other gangs will have control and we'll have nothing. Then they'll have us in their power. We'll starve if we just wait around. I say we start attacking on our own."

Lisa wanted to say something about that, but she forced herself to keep quiet.

"I think Lisa's right," said Julie.

Ah, Julie, thought Lisa. *Now* I forgive you.

Steve Cole had been nodding his agreement with Charlie, and now he spoke. "The fact is, we don't have *any* food. As Charlie says, there isn't any except the food that belongs to the rich kids. Their parents had pantries filled with canned things that they'd never eat. Yesterday I saw Janet Lester swimming in her pool. I'll bet she's got all kinds of extra food. Why not get it before the Chidester Gang does? It's not fair. Why should they have all that food, while we have none?"

Lisa thought, Well, there are two generals we can't trust—Steve and Charlie. But she still kept silent. She waited for Jill to speak. She respected Jill.

But Craig spoke instead.

"I've been thinking that we should grow food. We can

do it now; we don't have to wait till spring. I'm making a solarium. It's like a greenhouse, and we can raise vegetables in it, even in winter. We can live on vegetables. I know, because my dad told me about vegetarians. We can raise enough to get by."

Now we're getting somewhere, Lisa thought. She urged him on silently.

But then Jill spoke. "So what if you raise food? Are you going to share it with us? If your crop is bad, who gets what little there is left?"

"We do, Erika and I. But why can't you do the same? I don't mind teaching you how. With all those kids, you'd have plenty of gardeners."

Someone else said that they should try to make friends with the Chidester Gang. Another kid thought it would be a good idea to hire Tom Logan's gang. "We can give them food from your secret supply places, Lisa, and they can protect us. Why should we go to all the trouble of making our own militia?"

Lisa just had to speak now. "*We* can use *my* supply? *My* secret supply? No thanks, *I* will decide what's done with *my* supplies! You don't mind, do you?" She was mad again. It was time for her strategy.

"You're all worried about food. You say there isn't any, so you want to start a gang of thieves. But there are lots of other things you're going to need besides food. How about aspirin? Band-Aids? Soap? Matches? Flashlights? Charcoal? Toilet paper? Bactine? Vitamins? Seeds for your solarium? Where are you going to steal these things when all the supplies are used up? What good will stealing do, then or now?"

Lisa reached into her bag and pulled out a sample of almost every item she had named. Then she pulled out a Coke. "Who wants one of these?" And a handful of candy bars. "Who wants these?" Then she threw 10 packets of vegetable seeds on the ground—carrots, corn, pumpkins, beans, and some others.

She had shown enough. Their eyes widened as they stared at the treasures scattered at her feet.

"I know," she continued, "where to get hundreds of each of these items. My house is filling up with them. It's not because I'm lucky or because I'm some kind of special person. And it's not because I'm stealing. It's because I decided to use my head instead of crying or praying or forming a gang!"

She wasn't finished yet. "But I'm not sharing a thing, not a single thing. You can attack me if you want, but I'll burn it all before I let any thieves have it."

Her plan hadn't included getting angry, so Lisa relaxed her voice. It took a moment. "Craig is right. Soon we can survive by learning how to grow things. Until then, my sources will keep us alive. But I won't share anything until we all agree on a militia.

"For Craig's garden to grow or my ideas to work, we have to have protection against the gangs. When they run out of things to steal, they'll come after us. Someday, if we're smart, we'll be growing food and making things, and we'll learn how to survive forever without taking from anyone. But now we need a militia. It will give us time to use our heads and a chance to protect what we have. I'll share what I know with those who will support the militia."

She was finished. It seemed that her strategy was working. No one had any criticism.

"Any more discussion?" Lisa asked, hoping that there would be none.

"Then," she added, "I call for a vote. All those who promise to support the militia, stay here and we'll start to make plans. Those who refuse, go back to your homes."

Nobody moved. So it was agreed.

"Craig can be the commander of the militia," Lisa said. "Let's meet here again tomorrow at four, and Craig will present his plan for our defense. I'll help you, Craig. I have some ideas. Anyone else who has suggestions, please give them to Craig before the meeting. Also, will each house decide on an alarm and tell us what it is tomorrow?"

That was the end of the meeting. One of the children asked Lisa if there would be popcorn tomorrow. She smiled and said that there would be.

The Grand Avenue Militia was formed.

■

Lisa's mind was alive with ideas that night. Somewhere in the middle of her thoughts, Todd interrupted. "What does strategy mean, Lisa?"

She was too tired to be sure, but she answered. "Strategy is a plan for action that you think will work. If it does, it's a plan that is logical."

The word logical helped make it clear to him, and he asked, "What was your plan at the meeting?"

She explained that she had brought the popcorn to gain the children's confidence. Then she had let them run out of words before making her deal—food in exchange for a militia. Finally, to convince them that she wasn't just talking, she had shown what was in the bag as proof.

"To be free, you need protection against people who want to control your life. No one should tell you how to work or take what you have earned." Then she was too tired to say anymore.

"Good night, Toddy-boy. Tomorrow will be a busy day." Before she put her thoughts to rest, she remembered something else that was important.

Ever since the plague, she had been ignoring her friends and neighbors. She and Todd had created their own private world, and now she could see how dangerous that could be.

"They don't all see things the same way I do," she thought. "I should keep more in touch with them, or I could lose everything I've worked for."

She recalled Charlie's comments, and Steve's, and Jill's. Obviously, her ideas weren't obvious to everyone. That the Chidester Gang would steal and that her best friend would deceive her—these things proved that she needed to be a part of their society. Or at least she would have to keep her eyes and ears open and help to build their community into one that could protect her freedom.

All the brilliant ideas in the world would be useless

if that world collapsed around her and she was the only one left to steal from.

CHAPTER SIX

Lisa had to start by trusting someone. So she walked over to the Bergmans' house. Craig saw her coming and opened the door.

"Will you ride with me for supplies today, Craig?" she asked. "We can talk about the militia as we go." He made no comment. "Oh, and you can bring a list of things your family needs, because I think we're going to find a gold mine today. I mean a place filled with all kinds of supplies—almost everything we need."

She had used the right words. He agreed to come. "See you at nine," she said.

■

Craig was waiting nervously by the car. What's the matter with him? Lisa wondered as she approached. He didn't seem to notice her at all. His eyes were fixed on the scratched and dented body of the Cadillac.

"That poor car has been through a lot," she admitted, "but I'm a pretty good driver now. You'll see!"

That wasn't quite enough to reassure him. He's probably thinking some snotty things about women drivers, Lisa guessed as they both climbed in. From the corner of her eye, she caught him struggling with his seat belt. I'll show him! Concentrating hard, she steered the car smoothly out into the street.

"Still worried about my driving?"

"Just take it easy, Lisa!" Some of the paleness had already left Craig's face.

Lisa ignored the warning. "I have one source already that's pretty good. It might have enough food for the whole block to live on until spring, but I'm not sure." Lisa was speaking of the farms on Swift Road. "But today we're going to check out another idea I have. If I'm right about it, we'll find food and supplies to last for years. There might be other important things there, too, like medicine and tools.

"But first, Craig, you have to promise to keep my idea a secret, an absolute secret. If you help me on my trips, you can use the Secret Place to get whatever your family needs. I'll decide about sharing it with the other kids when I'm sure they'll support the militia. Okay?"

"Okay, but tell me where we're going. I can't leave Erika alone too long. And please slow down, Lisa, you almost hit that telephone pole!"

Big baby, she thought to herself. I wasn't even close

to that pole!

"Well, we're going to try to find . . . ." She hesitated, still not trusting him. "Do you promise, Craig, to keep this a secret? No matter what happens?"

He agreed, and she trusted him. After all, what choice did she have? Making the supply trips alone would be hard, and it wouldn't be safe for her to be away so much. With help, she could cut the time of each trip in half. And it would be good to have someone along for protection, even if it was Craig.

An important thought came to Lisa. "There's one other promise I'd like you to make, Craig. If something should ever happen to me, please promise to take care of Todd. It's a fair deal. My Secret Place can give you food to stay alive. All you have to do is keep my secret and be responsible for Todd if he ever needs help."

"Sure, it's a deal. I'll be your insurance policy for Todd. Now, please tell me about your big idea."

"Okay. We're going to try to find the Jewel Grocery warehouse on North Avenue. If my idea is right, it's full of millions of things we need." She looked at him. "If any place has lots of food and supplies, don't you think it would be a grocery warehouse?"

"Yeah, you're right. It's a great idea! But what made you think of it?"

"I don't remember exactly," she answered.

"Watch out, Lisa!" His warning came just in time as she swerved to avoid hitting a stray dog.

They drove east toward Elmhurst, slowly and in silence, and looked out at the streets they passed. There was no sign of life except for a few homeless animals. The stores and factories along North Avenue were deserted.

They wondered where the children of these neighborhoods had gone. Had they all moved away? What kind of life did they have now? How were they learning to survive? Someday, Lisa thought, when things were more secure, they might come back for a better look. But not today.

At Highway 83, Lisa and Craig stopped to study the map. Above them a dead traffic light watched over an empty intersection.

From the road, it was hard to read the numbers on the buildings. The fact that the warehouse would have a large "Jewel" sign painted on its front didn't occur to them until, happily, they saw the large blue letters. They had finally arrived.

To Craig's surprise, Lisa drove past the building and turned into a side street. She explained that it was important to hide their discovery by circling around on the back roads to the rear of the building. In front, the moving car would attract attention, and it would be stupid to lead the gangs to her treasure.

But her heart sank when she saw the broken second-story windows of the warehouse. They seemed proof that she hadn't been the first to think of the idea. Not so smart after all, are you? she chided herself. Her confidence faded. Angrily, she turned the car away.

"What are you doing?" said Craig. "Aren't you even going to look inside after coming all this way?" But she kept driving. "Stop, Lisa. Go back. We should at least look!" She stopped the car and glared at him.

"Lisa, look at that building over there. It's just an old factory, and *its* windows are broken, too. Maybe some kids just had fun breaking windows and never bothered to look inside. Look—the doors are still shut."

"Sorry, Craig. You're right. I guess it would be dumb not to look at least. We'll go back."

She turned the car around and drove back to the warehouse. Before Craig had unfastened his seat belt, Lisa was running toward the door of the building. It was shut tight. Good! And the lower windows were unbroken. Great! She picked up a large brick and ran along the outer wall, toward the nearest window.

"Wait, Lisa!" Craig's shout followed her. "Don't break in *there*. It will just make kids curious."

"And don't *you* shout!"

When he caught up with her, she said, "Okay, how about one of those windows over there behind the bushes?" He nodded, and soon they were smashing the glass of a large pane.

"Now go to the trunk of the car, Craig. Here are the keys. Get the box of tools. We're going to have to saw through these bars."

He walked back to the car and unlocked the trunk. Lisa had quite a collection of tools in there. Craig was impressed.

With a hacksaw, he began sawing vigorously at the hard steel bars. Lisa gave him an account of what she could see inside the building. "I see rows and rows of big boxes. I can't tell what they are, but I'm sure no one has been inside." The hacksaw was sharp, but it took at least an hour to cut the main bar in two places.

Craig slipped between the bars first and then helped Lisa up and through the window.

They walked in silence, not believing their eyes. What treasures they saw! There were tools, medicines, clothing, matches, candles, charcoal, flashlights, paper plates, can openers, soap, and all kinds of food. It seemed that everything they would ever need was in there.

For the next hour they wandered through the long, wide, crowded aisles, their flashlight beam piercing the darkness ahead of them. They ran from row to row. "Craig, look . . . over there!" He saw a hundred, maybe a thousand cases of canned pop stacked all the way to the ceiling. Lisa thought about all of the new friends she could make with those cans.

"Look over here!" and they tried to guess how many jars of peanut butter were in a stack of cases near the loading ramp.

"I didn't think there was this much soup in the whole world, Craig. Hey, I've got a deal for you. You can have all the cream of asparagus and I'll take the chicken noodle." Much to her surprise, he agreed. Weird kid, she thought. He actually likes cream of asparagus soup.

Looking at all that food made them hungry. "Let's eat!" Craig said as he pulled a can of pears from a box. She brought some potato chips out from a huge stack of cartons. They made a meal of pears, potato chips, and warm pop. Craig opened a second can of pears. It was sloppy fun to eat them with your hands.

While they ate, they talked about the potential of this Secret Place. How should they move and hide all these goods? No matter how they did it, they must keep the warehouse a secret. Craig understood now how important that was.

Lisa came up with a plan. "We'll take all the canned goods, and I mean every single can. They will last a long time, at least a year, I'm sure. Breakfast cereal and boxed-up stuff like powdered milk can't last forever, so we'll take only enough to last till spring."

She continued. "We've got to find several different places to hide the supplies in case one of the places is discovered. We'll put a supply of each item in each place."

For starters, they decided on six hiding places where the other kids were least likely to go: an empty hangar at the DuPage County Airport, the silo at the farm on Swift Road, the basement of Cottington's Furniture Store, and the furnace rooms of three churches in Glen Ellyn.

But as their plan unfolded, the fun and excitement gave way to hard work and realization of the danger ahead. They knew that their trips would have to be made at night in total darkness—there could be no car lights on the long drive down North Avenue. It was frightening.

"Lisa," Craig warned, "the militia meeting starts in one hour. We'd better get moving." They rushed to load the car with the things they'd never expected to have again—chewing gum, marshmallows, popcorn, pop, and candy bars.

"You drive home, Craig," Lisa said, as she climbed into the other side of the car.

Driving scared him at first, but he tried not to let it show. To make it easier for him, she said, "I learned by remembering the instructions my dad gave over and over when he taught my mother how to drive. He said them so many times that I learned them by heart."

Lisa recited the instructions while Craig guided the car slowly and clumsily out of the warehouse lot. "Look all around you . . . release the brake . . . easy on the gas . . ."

The car shot forward and demolished a trash can next to the warehouse. So, Craig thought, that's what she meant by "easy." The can did no damage to the car besides making another dent in the right fender. "This car is indestructible," he said.

As they drove away, Lisa looked back, not wanting to lose sight of the warehouse. It now seemed 100 times larger than when they had first discovered it.

The two children rode quietly for a long time, looking out at the wintry grayness. They thought about the Secret Place. The warehouse offered security and an end to their struggle against starvation. If they were smart and careful about moving and hiding their supplies, they might have a whole year to plan for the future.

At first Lisa had wanted to get even with Craig for his "back-seat driving," but she knew that it would be wrong to tease him now. Craig was a natural driver, and Lisa told him so. Besides, he was fun to be with. If they worked together, they would have a better chance.

Craig was the only older boy she knew. She thought she understood his fears, because they were the same as her own. It was good to understand someone that way.

Craig wanted to know about Lisa's other secret sources. When she explained about the farm on Swift Road and described the inviting note from the old lady, he became interested.

"You know, Lisa, if I could choose any kind of life in this mess, I think I would be a farmer. Growing things is a lot of fun. Let's go to that farm sometime. My father taught me a lot about gardening, and I know I could raise food. Wouldn't it be nice to stop looking for food and start *making* it instead?"

Lisa thought for a long time before answering. "Somebody has to grow food, that's true. But do you really want to hide away on a farm? I'd rather get the world back to the way it was, with schools, and hospitals, and electricity. See how important those things were?"

She paused, expecting him to say something. He kept quiet instead.

"Just think of the big jets at the airport," she continued. "Once they carried people thousands of miles away, and now they just sit there. They're useless.

"We've spent whole days trying to find food, and now we've found a big supply. Next, let's try to figure out a way to get things working again. I mean the jets and trains and things."

"Lisa, you're a dreamer. Don't you know that it takes years of training to fly a jet? Besides, there aren't any teachers left, so who would show us how? Books can't teach us that. Forget about it, Lisa. We're just kids."

How could she answer? He was probably right, but

would they have to live like the people in olden times, working all day in the fields? Or, even worse, would they end up like those children in really poor places, begging, stealing, and having no time for fun? Would they grow old and tired while the jets on the runway rusted away?

"Craig, I know it sounds crazy, but I think we can do it. We can make things work again. Sure, we're just children, but—" Her words, like her confidence, faded into confusion.

North Avenue was still deserted as they moved toward home. Where are the children? they wondered again to themselves. They drove without speaking from North Avenue to Swift Road, to St. Charles, then Riford, and then turned onto Grand.

The children were waiting in the street for the militia meeting and their popcorn feast. As the car moved into the driveway, they surrounded it. Without saying much, they opened the back doors and began unloading the cartons and boxes. They moved quietly, with sure steps. They knew exactly what they had to do. To Lisa and Craig, those children didn't seem like children any longer.

CHAPTER SEVEN

This is not my meeting, thought Lisa, grateful to Craig for taking charge. At the moment she was feeling too confused to be a leader.

Although Craig was describing his plan for the Grand Avenue defense, Lisa could see that his heart wasn't really in it. He wanted to farm, not fight. He needed peace and simple things instead of all this talk about war.

The other children were listening carefully. Tomorrow they would begin the work of setting up a different alarm system for each house. From the Glen Ellyn police station they would get guns and ammunition. They would pour gasoline into glass bottles to make bombs. Each house would collect a stray and train it as a watch dog. They would also gather an arsenal of knives, rocks, and other simple weapons.

After listening to Craig's plan, the children were no

longer afraid. They felt even better when they heard about the fantastic treasure in the Secret Place. Everything was going to be all right. They had plenty of food, and nobody would dare attack Grand Avenue.

Lisa studied their faces. Look what Craig has done for them, she thought. Erika looks as happy as she did on her last birthday. Even Julie is smiling.

Finally her eyes came to Todd's face, which had an altogether different look. He was staring down the street and turning pale. He pointed toward Chidester. She turned to look.

The Chidester Gang! There must have been 50 of them, mean looking and moving slowly toward the happy gathering. A few of the children screamed and ran away. The meeting was over.

"Wait!" Lisa ordered. "Stay here, and we'll see what they want. Don't run away! Don't look afraid!"

The gang stopped, and Tom Logan walked forward alone. "Lisa Nelson," he called out, "I want to talk to you." She stepped away from her group to meet him. "What do you want?" she asked, calm and strong.

"I'm Logan," he said, "and I've got a deal for you." He was the tallest and strongest kid in the Chidester Gang, and he didn't look at all afraid.

"Let's hear it," Lisa replied with a fearlessness that matched his. The children watched.

"I know that you've got all kinds of supplies. We don't know where you're getting them yet, but we'll find out—soon." He was threatening her.

"We could wipe you out right now and take everything you have, but we don't want to do that." He paused to make the threat sound more frightening. "We don't want to do that," he repeated. "You have the supplies and we have the army. I want to make a deal. We'll protect you with our army if you'll share your stuff with us."

Lisa said nothing and waited.

"There are other gangs, you know," Logan said, getting impatient. "These gangs are as strong as we are, and tomorrow—or tonight—they could wreck you. You need our help, and we'll give it to you in exchange for a share of your supplies."

Still she said nothing.

"Lisa, my sister was your babysitter for two years. She liked you, and I liked your family, too. We should cooperate. We can . . . ."

He knew she was waiting for him to say something else.

"Okay, Lisa," he said finally. "I'm sorry for what we did to Todd, but we had no choice. You can't run a gang without food. My boys were starving. I had to do it."

Now she understood him a little better. "Sorry, Tom, but I could never trust you or your gang. If you would betray a neighbor once, you'd probably do it again. At least I'd never be sure."

"Now wait a minute!" Tom wanted to defend himself, but it was still Lisa's turn to speak.

She went on. "We can take care of ourselves! You're right, we have supplies, more than you could ever dream of. Soon we'll have power too—a militia that could stop your gang any day. So go ahead. Take our things. You'll be wasting your time, because today there's not much here for you to steal. But by tomorrow or the next day, we'll have things that you will never have, because you're not smart enough to find them yourself. Just try to attack us then. You won't know what hit you!"

Don't get so emotional, she cautioned herself. She wanted to hurt him for hurting Todd.

"I don't blame you, Tom . . . really." Her words softened. "And I don't want any trouble with your gang. It's just that we don't need your help. We can take care of ourselves, and we will!"

The children were silent. What gave Lisa the courage to say those things?

Tom's confidence was shaken. He could scare them into an agreement, but there was something about her that stopped him. He walked away, saying nothing more. His gang followed him back to Chidester.

It took some time for the militia meeting to return to order. No one wanted what the gang offered, but they were uneasy about Logan's threats. They had food and supplies and a strong plan for defense, but still they worried.

"Anyone want some more popcorn?" Lisa asked, hoping that the old bribe would bring the meeting back to order.

"No thanks" was the general reply. The popcorn could be saved for another time. They began to ask a hundred questions about the Secret Place and the militia.

Lisa whispered to Craig. "Don't forget your promise. They must not know where the Secret Place is."

Craig nodded, thinking about Lisa. Sometimes she seemed a little crazy. "Don't worry, I'll keep the promise," he said. The whole day seemed incredible. This morning he was starving, and now he was the general of an army and an insurance policy for a little boy.

Lisa, even more than the other children, understood the day's importance. "Come on," she hollered above the many voices, "let's go to Lake Ellyn for a campfire. I've got a whole sack of marshmallows, and there's soda and chips in my trunk. Craig, help the boys get some wood to burn. We'll build a bonfire by the boathouse. You girls go get the blankets. Julie, get your boom box and some tapes. We've got batteries for it. Todd, give me a hand with the pop."

In a few minutes, Grand Avenue was empty. Every child happily joined the procession to Lake Ellyn. The bronze Cadillac led the way and 20 kids were following it, singing a Christmas carol.

They had almost forgotten about Christmas, and it was coming soon. When Eileen, one of Jill's kids, wondered if Santa would bring presents this Christmas, Lisa assured her that he would. There had been thousands of toys in the warehouse.

Lisa turned to Charlie. "Run back to your house and get all the Christmas tree decorations you can find," she said. This surprised him. It was still a little early for Christmas, but he did as she asked.

They had built a huge fire near the lake by the time Charlie came back with the box of ornaments. "What do you want these for?" he finally asked.

"What do you think? We're going to decorate a Christmas tree." But when Lisa carried the boxes to a pine tree near the fire, the children began fighting over the decorations. "Wait a minute! We can't all do it," Lisa said. "Katy and Todd will decorate the tree."

They sang all the Christmas carols they knew. There were a lot of them, because Julie had a fantastic memory for songs. The marshmallows were gone in no time, the fire was huge and bright, and the children laughed and sang and forgot about their problems.

It was just like the parties in the old days. They were children again, and life was fun.

Charlie, who had been more afraid than anyone, began to act like his old, mischievous self, teasing his sisters and making them mad. Even that was fun, except, of course, for Julie and Nancy. The children laughed until very late into the night. They hardly noticed the cold.

The moon was full and shining on the icy lake. Lisa wandered toward the shoreline to be alone for a moment. There were many problems to think about, and this would be a good time for thinking. What will happen to us? she asked herself, over and over.

But now she didn't fear the answer as much. It seemed that they were beginning to control their own futures. They would use their heads. That was the key.

"Lisa, is that you?" called Jill from her dark perch on the dock. "Come over here for a minute. There's something I want to talk to you about."

Lisa sat beside her. They listened, for a while, to the songs in the background. There was no hurry.

Lisa finally broke the silence. "What is it, Jill?"

"Well, I've got a problem, and I thought you might be able to help me. There are 14 kids at my place now and they eat like crazy. We just don't have enough food or supplies. Will you help us? We need lots of things, especially medicine. Some of the kids have bad colds. Do you have anything for us?"

Lisa knew that she could help them. In fact, she'd be happy to share the wealth of the Secret Place. But why should she, if Jill's kids wouldn't help with the militia?

"Okay, Jill, here's what we can do. I'll be happy to help you out, but not for free. I need someone for every hour of the day and night to walk up and down Grand Avenue. They'll alert us if an enemy approaches. I'll get my dad's trumpet, and the sentries can learn how to make a warning blast on it. But I'll need someone night and day, every day.

"Also, I'll need at least two of your kids to help Craig and me on our supply missions. It will take about four hours for each trip, but we'll probably go only three nights a week until January.

"If you'll agree to those terms," Lisa said. "I'll guarantee you and your kids all the supplies you need."

But Jill's awkward silence made it clear that she wasn't ready to accept the deal.

Finally she spoke. "Lisa, can you imagine what it would be like for a five-year-old to walk up and down Grand Avenue late at night, afraid of everything that moves? Can you imagine how scared they'd be? You and I are older. We can find the courage to do it, but they can't. I think it's cruel of you to demand it of them. They need our help. They're afraid, Lisa. Don't you remember what that's like?"

"Of course I remember, Jill," she replied. "I'm afraid almost every minute of the day, and so is Todd. He's not much older than your kids, but he's fighting that fear. He earns his way and it makes him happy and strong.

"We're still children, but we have to keep alive. Everything is different now. Those kids need the same things we do! They've got to *try,* too!"

But Jill wasn't listening. Even Lisa, when she thought about it, realized that she couldn't expect helpless children to join an army.

Lisa gave in, finally, but only because she couldn't put the facts together. Was she expecting too much of them? She started again.

"Okay, maybe you're right. Maybe I expect too much of everyone. But you have to understand the way I feel. Surviving isn't such a bad problem if we can just use our heads. In fact, we'll really have something when we know we've actually *earned* our survival. That's the way I felt today when we found the secret supply. Try to understand what I'm saying."

To Jill it sounded good, but the facts she faced every day didn't quite fit with Lisa's ideas. To Jill, life was just little orphans and the problems of finding food and medicine for them. Somehow, she just couldn't think of those real problems as fun or satisfying or as being part of a grand plan.

"Jill, you know that I'll help you," said Lisa. "There's

plenty for your kids in our Secret Place, and you're welcome to whatever you need."

Lisa didn't think much more about that conversation. She knew something was wrong, but she couldn't figure out what it was. Were her feelings so strange? Was all this struggling such a bad thing, or was it the key to their happiness? She wasn't sure.

She did realize one very important thing. Her ideas might bring them all a year of freedom from hunger. The warehouse, the car, the farm—all these ideas would help to save lives.

But it seemed that they all felt it was her duty to help them, and that what belonged to her was theirs also. Oh, well, they're afraid, she thought. I can understand that. Maybe I'm just lucky that all this craziness is a challenge for me.

■

In the warmth of their bed that night, Lisa tried to explain her feelings to Todd. Would he understand?

"At first, this whole mess scared me," she told him. "I thought we were going to starve. It was horrible just to stay alive.

"But then struggling began to seem like the best thing I had. What fun would it be if we were robots— if everything was automatic, and we couldn't change anything?

"Just think of a robot, Todd. It can't feel, or choose, or gain, or lose. It can't think, and it doesn't even know that it exists. Think what it would be like without any problems, Todd. Life would be dull. Sure, we have a lot of problems right now, but problems are really challenges, and they can make life exciting, if you're not afraid.

"I'm proud of my discoveries, even though it's true that anyone else could have found them. That's really true—anyone else could have done it.

"Todd, are you still awake?" He was. He had understood his big sister. He didn't ask for a story that night. Their life was becoming an adventure that was as good as any of her stories.

"Lisa," he said, "I'm glad you're my sister."

They went to sleep.

CHAPTER EIGHT

The week that followed was filled with activity. The plan was under way, and the children of Grand Avenue were excited.

Defense was important. Even the little kids could understand that now. The Chidester Gang and other gangs would try to capture their supplies. They had to be ready.

Julie and her family were training the watchdogs. The dogs would attack on command—at least that's what Charlie promised.

Each child-family had its own defense alarm. At Lisa's house, it would be Todd's trumpet. Craig's kids would use a loud whistle, and Jill's would beat a drum. The Harris' house would ring its old bell, which once had been heard for blocks at dinner time.

Grand Avenue sounded like a machine at work.

There were hammers, dogs, alarms, rock slides, and children shouting. But the gunfire was the hardest thing to get used to.

At nine each morning, Craig held target practice in the Triangle. Everybody older than five had to come. They fired small .22-caliber rifles at tin cans lined up along a low branch. Even though he didn't know much about guns, Craig was their teacher. The children all feared this part of the training, but they tried to learn.

It sounds like we're having a war, Craig thought. He wondered how many curious children from the other streets in the neighborhood would come over to check out the noise.

Each house adopted Lisa and Todd's idea of a rock slide on the roof. Lisa and Todd showed the others how to set it up with wire hangers and string.

Craig helped the family captains find bottles and gasoline to make Molotov cocktails. They were crude but impressive weapons. When thrown onto the pavement, they made a frightening explosion and burst into flames. Since there was no more gasoline at the gas stations, each house used the cans left for the lawn mowers in their garage. The children filled old bottles with gas and stuck rags in them to serve as fuses.

The militia captains from each house met with Craig every morning to discuss the day's plans. The captains left the briefings with drawings, tools, and all kinds of junk—rope, wire, tin cans cut up in odd ways, ladders, planks, and saws. They needed all this stuff for construction. Each captain had to modify the plans according to the special needs of his or her house.

Craig worked in Julie's basement because there were more tools available there. Charlie and Todd helped out in the shop. They reported for work at six each morning, and the three of them hammered and sawed furiously to get their contraptions ready for the captains.

"Darn it," Charlie said, whenever he hit his thumb with the hammer. Craig had stopped the swearing because he thought it was bad for Todd to hear it. He would have been surprised to hear Todd's own muttered words when he bumped his head on the work bench for the fifth time in one morning.

It was strange to see the change in the captains as the days passed. They were collecting a lot of bruises, but there were no major injuries. "Hey," Craig said, laughing, "we look like a real army with all these bandages, and we haven't even had a battle yet."

The Grand Avenue houses were turning into odd-looking fortresses. By the fifth day, there was an avalanche of rocks waiting to be triggered from each roof. A system of ropes and pulleys connected the houses, with a small mail pouch hanging from the rope to carry messages back and forth. Barbed wire looted from the hardware store was strung from one tree to the next, forming a barrier around the houses. The windows were boarded up with planks and shutters. Snarling dogs strained at their leashes, and warning signs were nailed everywhere.

Long, narrow boards stretched between the rooftops, forming a network of catwalks. "In case of a heavy attack," Craig explained, "it will be safer for us to be together in one house. We can climb across the houses to Julie's. We'll saw through the roof to make a trapdoor."

In the evenings, just before dark, the children had militia meetings. Each child chose his favorite weapon and practiced using it against imaginary enemies. They had knives and baseball bats and slingshots and spears. Craig made battle plans and drew maps of the block to plot their defenses.

Every day they had emergency drills. When a house alarm sounded, Craig timed the militia's response to see how fast the members could gather their weapons and rush to the house in danger. At first it was a mess, with children running in every direction. But after about 20 drills, they could assemble in less than four minutes.

After the first drill, while they were laughing at their confusion, Eileen, one of Jill's kids, came up with an idea.

"That was really fun," she said. "It's just like a fire drill at school." Then she suggested, "Why don't we get some fire extinguishers and squirt them at the bad kids? That would be more fun than shooting guns."

What made her think of that? They couldn't imagine, but it *was* a good idea. Craig sent a group of children to Forest Glen School to get a few. They soon returned loaded down with long, red cylinders that still worked. The shooting foam would at least confuse and slow down their attackers.

The ideas were working, and everyone on Grand Avenue was having fun. They were proud of their work, and many of them were beginning to share Lisa's feeling that working to survive and feeling proud of it could be a sort of happiness.

They were building a real community, and a pretty tough community, too. Each end of the street was blocked with barbed wire and growling dogs. A large sign stood by each blockade as a warning to intruders:

WARNING
Private Property.
Travel at your
own risk.

We want friends and peace.
We don't want to hurt you!

The citizens of Grandville.

They were ready, now. They all felt it.

◼

On the sixth day, Lisa and Craig decided it was safe to go back to the warehouse.

"It will be better to have two cars, in case one should break down," Lisa said. "I'd sure hate to walk all the way back. Do you think you can drive your dad's car, Craig?"

"I'll try," Craig answered.

That night, when all the houses were quiet, Lisa instructed the sentry: "Be especially alert tonight. We'll be back by midnight."

The two cars left the blockade slowly, without lights.

It was very dark; there was no moon at all. The sentry followed them with his eyes as far as he could, until they went over the hill on Riford.

Suddenly there was a loud crash from that direction. The sentry ran toward the top of the hill. There was silence again, and no sign of anything. He returned to his station.

In the front car, the girl's thoughts were racing.

What a dumb thing to do, scraping the side of that parked car. I'll bet Craig's getting a big laugh out of that. Oh, well . . . I hope the warehouse is still our secret . . .

What should we get this trip? Toddy's been quiet lately . . . maybe I should take him along next time. It's cool how happy everyone seems to be now. I hope we won't need to fight anymore. Maybe we'll look so strong that no one will even bother to try. When we get all six supply places filled, then . . . then, we can start to plan for raising food. We'll need to know more about medicine and first aid. What if someone gets wounded? I wonder what Craig is thinking now.

She slammed on the brakes to let a cat cross the road. The screeching sound from behind told her that Craig wasn't paying attention. She instantly stepped on the gas to avoid the crash, but not in time. There was a loud scraping noise as his car struck hers. They stopped and got out of their cars to inspect the fenders.

"Not too much damage, I guess," Lisa said. "Just another couple of dents. Before long, Craig, your car will look as bad as mine."

Craig just stood there.

She continued. "Relax, it's no big thing. Just don't drive so close next time." Craig said nothing. They got back into their cars.

He was still a little shaken by the accident, but soon his thoughts turned to other things.

I hope that no one else has found the warehouse. I have to look for garden seeds while we're there. What a dumb thing to do, hitting her like that . . . dad would really be mad if he could see what I've done to the car.

I hope we never have to fight anyone . . . why should I be in charge of the militia? We're just asking for trouble. Sure, we say we're doing it just for defense, but what's to stop Charlie from provoking a battle? Maybe Lisa will find another general . . .

I can't wait to see the farm that she talked about. It would be fun to have a place like that and raise food. I'm not a coward. I know we need some protection, but we're getting carried away with the whole thing. Those kids think it's all great fun now . . . play-fighting and shooting guns and planning strategy. Just wait until they see some of their own blood. It's been fun building some of those traps and stuff, but . . . .

It was very dark. As they drove, they thought about their problems and the days ahead.

Craig was thinking of his farm, his fields, and his acres of crops. *I'll be the general for a little while, until I can train someone else to take over. But who?*

Lisa's car was barely visible ahead. Now and then her brake lights would flash a warning to him. Otherwise, it was dark.

We don't need to start all over, Lisa thought. *If we try hard enough, I'm sure we can figure out how to get some of it working again. Maybe not the jets, at least not for a long time, but for sure the power and water and . . . I don't want Craig to get too serious about that farm. The others can raise food. I need him to help me rebuild things. He's bright, and I'll need all the help I can get . . .*

There were so many things to be done—important things like setting up a new hospital. Of course, it would all take time, but they had to do it. Knowing how to raise corn wouldn't help remove a bullet from a kid's leg.

But maybe Craig was right. Lisa wished she could put her feelings into words, but she didn't know the words tonight. Her mind was confused. It couldn't focus on anything but the black road ahead. Something, somewhere was wrong. She could sense it.

Their eyes were getting sore from following the faint white dashes painted on the highway. Finally, they reached the warehouse. It hadn't changed.

"Bring the flashlight," she whispered, as though their normal voices would carry all the way back to Chidester Street.

It was hard work loading supplies into the two cars. By ten they were exhausted, but the work continued for another hour. They had packed only essential items, the things that would save their lives. That's what they had decided. "Chips and pop won't save our lives," she said. "Leave them for another time . . . cough medicine is important, take it . . . and get some Bactine while you're in that section, aspirin too, and Band-Aids."

"Don't you think we should bring a few treats, Lisa? How about some candy bars?" They found some and added them to the other supplies, but there wasn't time for them to have a treat themselves. Lisa felt the urge to have a serious talk with Craig. But it would have to wait.

The clouds parted, and the moon lit the road on their ride home. They drove 10 miles per hour, then 20. Their tired bodies were anxious for rest, so they drove still faster.

Why is she going so fast? Craig wondered, as his speedometer hit 30.

The road was positively straight, and nothing lay in their path. Even the stray dogs were sleeping now.

He wanted to honk the horn or flash his lights as a warning for her to slow down, but he couldn't take any chances.

She's crazy, he thought, as he let her speed away from him. She must be going at least 50. She'll kill herself! He slowed down a little.

And then *he* decided to speed up. It was easy to control the car, especially when he stayed in the middle of the road. He wasn't going to let her beat him.

When the needle reached 60, he could see her just ahead. His hands were frozen to the wheel, his muscles tense. Pulling wide to the left side of the road, he roared past her at Main and Lombard.

She came up beside him at Highway 53, and together they slowed for the Swift Road turnoff. Lisa resumed the lead, and they went back to their snail's pace. A straight road was one thing, but the sharp turns on Swift Road were something else.

The excitement of the race was gone in an instant when they turned onto Grand and saw the street filled with children.

"What happened?" Lisa asked the sentry.

The Chidester Gang had attacked. "They must have heard you crash on Riford. That *was* you, wasn't it? They probably saw you leaving and knew it would be a good time to strike."

"Was anyone hurt?" she asked.

"No," he said, "nothing serious. They hit me on the head and then went straight for your house. Todd sounded the alarm and pulled the rock slide cord. The dogs were useless. They just wanted to play. But the rock slide did the job. A rock hit Tom Logan and knocked him out. The gang thought he was dead. They started carrying him away.

"Only four kids showed up right away. I guess the rest were afraid. By the time the other kids answered the alarm, it was all over. Most of them watched from behind the trees until they thought it was safe to be brave.

"By the time they got near my station, Tom was standing up. His head must have hurt a lot. The gang started to come at me but he called them off.

"I watched them leave. At first, I was afraid that we'd killed Logan. I don't like the kid much, but still, we don't want to kill anyone, do we?"

Lisa's little brother was the center of attention. The

other kids were coming over to give him high-fives. Todd was just glad to see his sister. He told her the story again in a rush of words. Lisa listened with new interest. He wasn't quiet anymore. He was excited, proud, and scared all at the same time.

"You're a brave boy, Todd. Just think of all you saved. They would have taken everything."

Lisa wanted to ask the other kids something: Where did their bravery go? Would they have stayed behind those trees while the gang beat Todd up again? What if that lucky rock hadn't found Logan's head?

But they were afraid. She could understand that.

The members of the Grand Avenue militia all wanted to share the credit. Before long, they were inventing new versions of the battle. The defense system they had slaved for was now the real hero. "It worked!" they shouted. "Our defense plan worked!"

The children were proud and more confident now. Let them imagine it as they please, Lisa thought. Maybe next time the memory will feed their bravery.

She knew that there *would* be a next time, but she was certain also that next time victory would not be a matter of luck.

Craig brought out the treats. Charlie built a bonfire in the street, and someone tried to make up a song about their "Grandville." Julie made up the new lyrics:

> *When we first came to this land,*
> *We were not so happy then,*
> *So we built a fighting band.*

Now we do what we can,
And we call our land
The land of Grand—
Grandville—Grandville.

They sang it over and over until it actually began to sound like a real song. It would run through their heads for hours.

Lisa ended the evening with a special announcement: "Let's declare that tomorrow will be the first holiday in Grandville. Sleep late if you like, but let's meet by the lake at noon." They roared approval and sang their new song all the way to their doors.

CHAPTER NINE

The melody still ran through Lisa's head as she climbed into bed next to Todd. "You were a brave guy, Toddy-boy. Will you come with me tomorrow night to the Secret Place? I need your help. Craig and I should take turns going, so that one of us will always be around here."

It was the best reward she could have given him. "You mean in the car and everything? Sure, Lisa, I'll come!"

"There's one other thing, Todd. I'd like to have you try to drive the car. We can practice tomorrow in the Glenbard parking lot."

Todd was a happy kid. His thoughts raced as Lisa drifted into sleep. What time is it? he wondered. What day is it tomorrow? How many days have gone by since we were left alone? He couldn't be sure, but it seemed to him that it had been a long, long time.

Even though it was an official holiday, the Grand Avenue citizens couldn't sleep late. At eight, a small band of children decided to form a wake-up party. They called on Julie first, then woke up Charlie and his sisters. At the Jansens', they added Jill, Missy, Katy, and all of their orphans. Then they went on to Steve and Cheryl's house. Steve was angry at first, but the cheerful procession was too inviting, so he joined in.

The mischievous troop went next to the Bergman house. "Let's scare 'em," said Steve. They surrounded the house, scratched lightly on the boarded windows and, on the count of ten, broke into a roar of war cries and giggles.

"You didn't scare us," Erika lied.

Craig was too sleepy to care. "Go away," he said.

"Come on, let's get Lisa and Todd," someone shouted.

The Nelson fortress was stronger than any of the others, so they walked over the rooftops from Craig's. "Be careful," he warned, as they tiptoed one by one across the narrow planks above the houses. "Quiet, you'll wake them!"

Craig had already made them walk those high planks during militia practice. "You can't be afraid," he had said over and over again, but the children were still scared. Some of the younger ones had cried, while the older children pretended to be brave. But today they all had courage.

"We'll slip down through the trapdoor," he whispered. "I'll go first and help you in. This will be a 'quiet' exercise. Remember, not a sound." He opened the padlock with his key.

It was strange to see 30 children on top of the house, disappearing, one at a time, into the roof. Amazing, thought Craig, how quiet they can be when they want to be.

Someone slipped on the trapdoor ladder and said a very bad word. "Quiet!" was Craig's whispered order. "Watch your step."

Eileen giggled a little too loudly at the bad word. The other children glared her into silence. It was a good thing that Lisa and Todd slept way down in the basement.

They tiptoed single file down the stairs, through the kitchen, and down to the windowless room in the basement. No one shouted. Julie knocked on their door. "Surprise! Wake up!"

Yawning heavily, Lisa could only say, "How did you get in here?" Todd's sleepy eyes tried to focus on the faces at the door.

They dressed quickly while the other children gathered tools and weapons for the day. Everything was loaded into the two cars.

"Drive slow," Charlie pleaded, "so I can ride on the hood."

"Hey, good idea," said Steve, and some of the other children climbed on top of the cars. The smaller ones piled inside. They drove toward the lake, followed by the shouts of those who were left to walk.

It was a great day, sunny and warm for December. Jill took the little ones to the swings, while a group of girls sat by a campfire singing. Charlie, Craig, Steve, and a half-dozen younger boys played football until the sky clouded up.

It turned cold when the sun disappeared. The whole party moved into the boathouse. Why hadn't they thought of it before? It was perfect. In no time the big fireplace was glowing. They laughed and sang for hours.

"Where are Lisa and Todd?" someone asked, noticing that they were gone.

"They'll be back soon," said Craig. He'd promised not to tell anyone that she was teaching Todd how to drive the car in the Glenbard parking lot. But Craig's answer made them suspicious. Before long the parking lot was filled with spectators and eager students. "It's not hard, really," some of them bragged. "Toddy is getting really good. Look at him now!"

Before long, Steve Cole approached them. "It's time for someone else to be the sentry. I've been on guard since noon, you know!"

"Here, Steve, want to try driving?" asked Lisa. "I'll show you how." He learned quickly. Good, she thought. Soon we'll have six or seven cars running.

After Steve's lesson, she called them all together. "Okay, let's pack up and get home. Hurry, it'll be dark soon. Let's load them up!"

Their first holiday was over. "They'll never be as good as this again," she said, and the children agreed.

After dark, Lisa and Todd got ready for their trip. "Keep a careful eye out tonight," she told the sentry. Lisa drove away, but not on Riford this time. Instead they circled around on Elm and Main, and then drove back to St. Charles at Five Corners.

Lisa's old doubts were nagging at her, but she didn't want to think about them. The celebration had really been fun, but something was wrong. What was making her feel so uncertain?

Lisa stopped the car.

"Toddy-boy, do you want to drive for a while?" Before he took over, she explained the instruments on the dashboard and the rules for night driving.

"Why can't we turn on the lights?" he asked, even though he already knew the answer. He strained his neck to see the road above the steering wheel.

"Here, Todd, you'd better sit on something so you can see." She folded their coats and added the pillow from the back seat. "There, is that better?"

Lisa coached her new chauffeur. "Easy on the brakes . . . turn the wheel slowly . . . don't jerk it . . . Todd, I said easy on the brakes!" But he was driving the car, a little boy. Was it possible?

"I didn't hit anything at all, Lisa," he said proudly, as he finally parked by the warehouse.

"You did a great job, Toddy-boy." What else could she say after all the dents she had put in the car?

"Please don't call me that, Lisa." He didn't mind the name before. But he was too big for it now. "Okay, Todd," she promised.

He was excited about the Secret Place when he saw it. He wanted to wander through it all night with the flashlight, but she interrupted his thoughts. "Come on, Todd, we've got a lot of work to do." They lifted, carried, and packed for two hours.

He slept all the way home. It's nice to have him along, Lisa thought. The little guy is really strong. We were lucky last night. The Chidester Gang could have wiped us out. He's brave, too.

Still, it *had* been luck. That rock falling on Logan was pure chance. It could have just scratched or bruised him and made him mad. He might really have hurt Todd . . . and that cowardly militia! She had to figure a way to toughen them up.

As the car turned onto Swift Road, Lisa thought, "No, not tonight. Surely they wouldn't attack again tonight." She reassured herself. "They're bound to think that Grand Avenue will be on a total alert . . ."

But she was wrong, very wrong. The next thing she saw was a giant flame reaching high above the trees. From as far away as St. Charles Road, she could see the terrifying glow.

"Todd, wake up! Todd, Todd!"

"What's the matter, Lisa?" He looked up and saw their home burning like a torch.

Then came the tears. The two children parked and got out of the car. They stood shaking, silently, in front of the home they'd always loved. They cried to themselves, as motionless as statues, while the blazing heat dried their tears.

"Come on, Lisa. Come on, Todd," the other children said. "Nothing can be done to save it now." But they didn't hear. They just stood and watched.

"There's nothing you can do, Lisa," said Jill. "You and Toddy-boy come home with me now. We have room. Please?"

"Toddy-boy?" He snapped out of his trance and turned around. "Who said that? My name is Todd . . ."

Lisa wasn't paying attention. "Why?" was all she could say, over and over, in her mind. "Why?" It was more than just the house. Her confidence and her joy and her wanting to rebuild things began to leave her. Her dreams and plans were being destroyed with the house.

She stood there, feeling nothing, through the night. Todd stayed beside her. The flames became embers, and the daylight finally shone upon them.

Then they went to Jill's.

PART TWO

HAVING THINGS IS SOMETHING,
BUT NOT EVERYTHING.

EARNING THE VALUES FOR
YOUR LIFE IS MORE
THAN JUST SOMETHING,
IT'S EVERYTHING!

CHAPTER TEN

What's the matter with Lisa? they all wondered. She just sits there thinking.

Actually she didn't think about much during that next week. Sometimes she would wander by the lake, and other times she'd talk to Todd, usually at night, in their bed. But most of the time, Lisa did nothing.

Her thoughts were all jumbled. I'm such a fool, she said to herself. I talked about changing things, and now things have changed me. I thought I could do anything, and I made such a big deal out of what I *would* do. Just look at me now. I'm just another orphan.

Jill had to take care of her. She was patient, and that's what Lisa needed most of all.

But the other children couldn't understand Lisa's reaction to the fire. She had faced much bigger problems and hadn't been discouraged. Why now?

Lisa thought about it too, and began to form an answer for herself. She still wanted to believe in the things she used to talk about. Before the fire, everything had seemed very simple to her. "Why not?" used to be her confident answer to anyone who questioned a wild plan of hers. When the old problems had come up, she knew what had to be done. But now she doubted her ability to think clearly. She doubted herself. So she waited and thought.

Lisa became more and more interested in Jill's children. They liked Jill for her kindness. And she really was kind to them.

Still, there was something wrong, something that was troubling them. They didn't play as they had in the old days. Instead they wandered about and whined for attention or treats. They wanted to feel useful. Lisa could sense it by the way they smiled whenever they had a new idea. "Jill, let's make a garden," one of them had said. "The flowers will make everybody happy."

Jill would say, "Yes, we'll do that in the spring when it's warm."

One boy invented a weapon out of woodscraps he'd nailed together. Jill told him, "You have a good idea there. Show me how it works." And she patiently watched him demonstrate it.

But it seemed to Lisa that the children quarreled too much. They fought constantly over their toys. There were enough toys so that each child could have at least two or three, but they all clamored for the same, beat-up, popular ones. The more Jill told them to share, the more they all seemed to need one particular toy for themselves. Even Jill lost her temper now and then when her words about sharing were ignored.

Sharing? Maybe that's part of the problem, Lisa thought one morning. An idea roused her into action.

Maybe what these kids needed was to have at least one toy they could call their very own. Lisa gathered the children together and tried assigning toys. But it didn't work; they still demanded the same old favorites.

Jill came in from the yard. "What's going on in here?" she asked. She didn't like Lisa changing her rules around. Jill thought sharing was an important thing. She *knew* it was!

Lisa sensed Jill's annoyance. She wanted to make peace but wasn't sure how to do it.

Lisa turned to the children. "Well, assigning toys isn't going to work, but I think I have a better idea. Listen carefully."

They listened, glad to see Lisa put aside her grief. "I think you should each have a new toy, one that is yours for keeps." They agreed, of course. "But since there are no more toys here, you'll each have to work to earn one." They were all willing to work.

Jill started to interrupt but stopped. She too was happy to see something other than sadness in Lisa's eyes.

Lisa continued. "You know how important it is for us to have cars to drive. They help us get food and many other things from the Secret Place. But soon the cars will be out of gas. We need more, and you can help us." The children looked puzzled.

"Do you remember how your moms or dads used to mow the lawn? Didn't they start by pouring gas from a can into the lawn mower? And wasn't that can a red-colored one? And don't you think it's probably still sitting in your garage?

"Okay, here's the deal." Lisa's old enthusiasm was back. "I'll have a nice new toy for you if you can find a can of gasoline and bring it here."

Some of them were already running for their coats. "Wait a minute, there's one more thing." They stopped to listen. "We will also be needing more cars soon. If you can bring me your parents' car keys, you'll get a very special extra reward. A whole box of candy for you alone, just you. Do you remember what their keys looked like? You might find them in your mother's purse or on your dad's dresser.

"Now, divide up into teams of two and be careful. If you can't find a gas can in your garage, then try a neighbor's. Jan, you take Beth . . . Bill and Larry, go together . . . Nancy, help Eileen . . ."

The children had a real project now. They hurried to get out and get started. "Where are my boots, Jill?" . . . "Who took my purple scarf?" . . . "I can only find one mitten."

Jill reminded them to be careful and hurry back.

After they had gone, Jill turned to Lisa. "They like your idea, but I'm not so sure that we should stop teaching them to share their things with each other. Sharing is very important, you know."

"I've been watching your kids for days, Jill. Just

watching and thinking about them. They do *too much* sharing and it isn't working at all. They have nothing of their own—no real duties, no real way of helping. It's nice to share things if you want to. But it's stupid to *force* people to share or to be nice. Those are things people have to do on their own. Otherwise it's no good. See what I mean?"

Jill didn't agree, but she didn't want to argue.

"You do all the work, Jill, and they hardly help at all. They wander about, whining for something to do and fighting over toys. You're really patient and good to them, but I think they need to have jobs and things of their own."

Now Jill was ready to argue. "But Lisa, they're afraid, really scared. You should hear them at night, the bad dreams and all."

"Yes, I've heard them," Lisa said. "I told you I've been watching your kids. All night long you seem to run from one child to another, trying to soothe them back to sleep. But when do *you* sleep? You look awfully tired, Jill."

"What can I do?" Jill really did want to know.

"I've told you what I think already. The children are afraid because they have nothing, nothing at all. It was bad enough for them to be orphaned, but it's even worse for them to be without their own . . . uh . . . personalities." Lisa couldn't think of the right word, and Jill misunderstood.

"Lisa, they have nice personalities and each one is different. What do you mean?"

"Well, I can't remember the word, exactly, but what

I mean is that . . . ah . . . well, I don't think they'll ever be happy if you do everything *for* them. They need to work and to be proud of themselves. They need to be able to say to themselves, 'I worked hard and did a good job and I *earned* my toy.'

"Don't you see?" she asked. "And it would make your job so much easier."

"Maybe you're right, Lisa, but I still think they're too young and too scared."

Lisa wanted to say something about how she had lost her own fear by solving problems and staying busy. It seemed to her that fear was how you felt when you waited for something bad to happen, and fun was what you had when you figured out a way to make something good happen.

She wanted to say these things, but how could she? She had been a victim of her own fear since the fire. She had turned into just another one of the scared children that Jill took care of.

"By the way," Jill said, "where are you going to get those toys you promised them?"

"That's simple," Lisa answered. "Tonight when Craig makes his supply trip, he can get some. They aren't really fancy toys, but they'll do. The Secret Place has hundreds of them. I guess we just forgot all about play. Doesn't it sound strange, Jill, to think of playing with toys?"

Instead of answering, Jill asked, "What is the Secret Place anyway, Lisa? It sounds so mysterious. Where is it?"

Lisa wanted to tell her, but she said, "You know I can't tell you, Jill, or anyone else. I can't risk having it discovered. If I told everybody, and the Chidester Gang really wanted to find out about it, all they'd have to do is torture someone into telling. The fewer people who know, the safer it is."

"Would you tell if they tortured you, Lisa?" Jill hoped she would say no.

"I don't know, Jill. I hope not."

Lisa was feeling much better now that some activity had brought her back to life. The children would be gone for another half hour or so. She asked Jill to call a quick meeting of the militia leaders. "Ask them to get over here right away."

Charlie, Steve, Craig, Todd, and Jill faced Lisa in the living room of Jill's house. She's back to her old self, they thought, as she rattled off a long list of new militia plans.

"Our defense plan is a joke," she said. "We've got to train those dogs to do more than just slobber on the enemy. And we've got to make our kids tougher. They're afraid to shoot or hurt anyone.

"Where was our brave militia when my house was being burned? Watching the flames from behind the trees? What if Todd had been inside? Let's make more Molotov cocktails and use them next time."

Was her audience deaf? They sat quietly listening to her angry words. Don't sound too violent, she cautioned herself.

And for no other reason than to change the subject, she started talking about her old ideas—the rebuilding plans, the first-aid stations, and other more fantastic dreams. But she realized that she didn't believe in them anymore. As if in a trance, she repeated the old plans mechanically, without enthusiasm.

Charlie stopped her. "Lisa, you're crazy! Forget all that junk, and let's talk about the militia."

His words stung her. Even though she too was giving up on all those plans, the way he talked to her made her angry. "Crazy, Charlie? Who's crazy? Shut up, Charlie!"

She stood up. "Go ahead, big militia captains. Make your plans!" She stopped herself. In a soft voice, she added, "You can do it. I know you can.

"I'm going for a walk," she said at the door, and left.

She walked to the shores of Lake Ellyn and sat on a bench. Crazy? she wondered. Maybe I am crazy . . . or am I just sick? I feel so tired, it's as if I had a sleeping sickness of some kind. But I've got to get control of myself. I've got to face the problems. Charlie was right about that. Forget the big dreams for now and solve today's problems.

Her mind began to clear. She listed the real dangers, but she could finally see that what they had to fear was much bigger than the Chidester Gang. What good would it do to build an army and add more weapons? How would that help when Tom Logan decided to join forces with other gangs? It was sure to happen sooner or later.

She imagined the other Grand Avenue houses burning to the ground one by one. She could see the "Grandville" citizens tortured and forced to give up their treasures in exchange for their lives. Finally, with no choice left, they too would have to join that army.

It was clear that Grand Avenue would be impossible to defend. What they needed was a castle with high walls and a moat, like in the days of King Arthur.

Her fear was dissolving away. She could see clearly now and her confidence was coming back. She would figure something out.

She walked to the lake past the boathouse. At the end of the dock, she sat down. I'll figure something out, she repeated over and over again, as if the words themselves would trigger an idea.

A castle with high walls, she thought, and then Lisa looked up. There it was, *right before her eyes*. A hundred times she'd looked up there and not seen it!

Glenbard, the old fortress of a high school, stood proudly, high on a hill. Its walls were tall and made of brick! The field and the lake were below it. A steep hill descended to Crescent Boulevard on the far side.

It was their castle, all right! Twenty children could defend it against 100, maybe 200 soldiers. There were big rooms for the families, classrooms, and the nurse's office for a first-aid center. There were kitchens, meeting rooms, sports equipment, art supplies, woodworking tools, indoor garages—and who could tell what else? Best of all, there'd be a library filled with books.

"Everything except a moat," she said out loud. "I've got it! I've got it!" Laughing and shouting, Lisa ran all the way around the castle and then home to tell the others.

The Jansen house was noisy with activity. As she approached it, she saw little workers bringing gasoline cans into the garage. "Here, Lisa, I found two cans. Can I have my toy?" "Here's some gas, Lisa, and I found these keys. My dad had two cars."

"Nice work. Put the cans in the garage. Any more car keys? Bring them to me."

Eileen was crying. "Lisa, I couldn't find any gas, but here are the keys. My daddy never brought the car home since he was sick. Are trucks okay? I think trucks are neat, and they can carry lots of things. But I couldn't find any gas." She started to cry again.

At that moment, Lisa didn't really care. "Trucks, Eileen? Where?"

"Oh, my dad's garage is on Geneva Road. It's really big. He made roads. There are dump trucks, too, and bulldozers, and stuff like that. Don't you like bulldozers, Lisa?"

The little girl couldn't understand Lisa's serious look, and she started to cry again. "I still get the candy, don't I?"

"Sure you will, Eileen. But trucks, wow! Can we ever use a truck! Thank you, Eileen. Thanks a lot. Will you show me how to get there sometime?"

"Uh-huh."

Missy had been watching them intently. She hadn't seen Eileen cry much before this. Missy came toward her and said, "I already have my can, but I think I know where another one is. Come on, I'll show you."

They ran off happily. Now, that's sharing, Lisa thought.

As she entered the house, she could hear loud arguing in the living room. Obviously, the militia meeting was still under way.

"It will never work," Craig was saying to Charlie.

"Hey, Lisa," Steve said. "Guess who's got the wild ideas now? You ought to hear Charlie's plan. Tell her, Charlie."

Lisa flopped down on the big couch. "I told you he was the crazy one," she said.

But Charlie wasn't a quitter. He described how they could train dogs to fight and kill if necessary. His dad had a book on training police dogs, and he'd read a mystery story about a man who trained killer dogs. Lisa was thinking about their castle surrounded by angry dogs. It would be even better than a moat, she thought.

Charlie noticed her smile and thought she was mocking his plan. "I'm not finished yet, Lisa," he said coolly. He went on to tell them that German shepherds were the best breed for the purpose. Since there were so many stray dogs everywhere, he was sure he could find dozens to train. "Besides, I know a lot about dogs. My dad taught me." Charlie had been secretly training Danny, his English setter. He offered to give Lisa a demonstration.

"That's not necessary, Charlie," she said. "I think it's a great idea. It's better to use dogs for fighting than children."

Then she decided to shock them. "And they'll be useful at the castle."

"What castle?" All of them said it at the same time.

"You thought my other ideas were wild, did you?

Wait till you hear this one!"

They listened carefully as she presented the details of the plan. There were no smiles and no jokes, just nodding. They could see her point that the houses on Grand Avenue were spread too far apart and were too hard to defend. The fire had taught them a lesson. Their own houses might be next.

She had expected them to argue and say that they wouldn't leave their homes. But they were excited.

"When do we start?" Jill asked.

"Tonight, of course!" Lisa answered. "There's no time to waste. We'll have to spend some nights under cover getting the place ready. Then, in about five or six days, we can move in. Eileen's dad had some big trucks. We'll figure out how to drive one and then, one night, we'll load all our stuff into the truck and slip it into Glenbard."

They worked over the details of the plan until dark. No one but the six plotters would be told a thing about it until everything was ready. In the meantime, Steve could learn to drive a truck, Lisa and Jill could plan the indoor city, and Craig and Todd could hide supplies. They would work at night, and Charlie would be the temporary defense captain. Somehow, in the meantime, they would keep the enemy away.

There was no crying in the Jansens' house that night. Could it be, wondered Jill, that earning their own toys is the reason for it? For once, Jill rested well.

But Todd and Lisa had far too many exciting thoughts for sleep. Lisa wanted her brother to understand why she was so happy. But how could she say it so he would understand?

A story seemed the best way. The setting for her story came to her easily.

Once there was a tiny kingdom across the sea with knights in shining armor who had lots of adventures. Everybody was truly happy. They were busy doing things they liked.

In a huge castle overlooking the sea lived the king and his young son, the prince. Their kingdom was very rich, because the king was the wisest man in the world—well, at least in their world. He knew how to be happy and he knew how to make his subjects happy. He was fair and generous, and most of all, he let his people be free.

Now you know from other fairy tales that kings usually made their money by taxing the people in their kingdom. Well, not this king—and maybe that was part of his wisdom. Other kings demanded cattle and gifts and jewels just because they wanted them. But they gave nothing in return. They didn't really think that peasants were as good as royal people.

But this king was really a lot like a smart businessowner. He thought of his subjects more as customers than as slaves. And since he was wiser than anyone—since he knew more than any ten of them put together—well, what I'm getting at is that he sold them his wisdom. When they were unhappy or when they had a problem, they came to him for advice. If he could solve their problem, which he almost always did, then they would have to pay him. He would charge according to the size of the problem.

Advice about farming, for example, would only cost a goat or a pig. But advice about how to be happy was his specialty, and because happiness is the most important thing in the whole world, he charged a lot more for that kind of advice. Usually the people paid with their best jewels or with a year of service as a soldier to defend the country against the other kings—the ones who thought it was easy to get rich by fighting and looting.

The other kings couldn't figure it out. Why was this king so rich? It seemed crazy to let his subjects be free and to organize an army that they didn't have to join.

But those kings never saw the stream of people in line to buy the king's advice. He got smarter and richer all the time. And the happier and freer his people became, the harder they worked. The harder they worked, the wealthier they became. The wealthier they became, the more time they had to face and solve their problems. And here was the king's secret: while he got smarter, they got richer, so he could keep raising his prices.

Everybody got happier and happier, and the king couldn't complain because he was getting richer.

But there was a big mystery about the king's happiness advice. The people swore on their very happiness, never ever to reveal what the king told them—ever!

Such happiness was everywhere. Maybe that's why they called it the kingdom of Real Fun. All the people of the land had real fun doing whatever they liked to do.

Does this sound a little too happy? Well, even the king had problems. Wisdom can't stop them altogether, you know.

Everybody was getting happier each day, except for one very sad person who became sadder every day. And it troubled the king greatly, because that sad person was the prince, his son!

Now the king's wisdom just wasn't great enough to deal with this problem. He tried everything to make the boy happy. He gave him horses and friends to play with and toys and servants. The boy didn't have a stitch of work to do. He had every reason to be happy, but he wasn't.

The king was smart enough to know that the sad prince could never rule the land, because he was learning neither wisdom nor happiness.

The more the king gave to the prince, the sadder the prince became. Before long, even the king himself started to become sad. I must not be so smart, he said to himself, if I can't even make my son happy.

When he was nearly at his wits' end, the king decided to get help. He offered a big reward and had a notice posted all over the kingdom.

"Whoever can tell me how to make my son happy," said the notice, "shall inherit this kingdom *upon my death."*

And it was signed: *"The King of Real Fun."*

As you might imagine, no one could advise the king as he wished, though hundreds of people tried.

And then tragedy came to the king. In the middle of a night that was sadder than most, the little prince disappeared. He was gone, without a trace.

Things got much worse, in fact, before they got better. The king began to lose confidence in his own wisdom and, of course, the advice business began to slack off.

Finally, one day in the spring of the second year after the prince had disappeared, business was so slow that only one person came to the king for advice. The king could see it clearly now. He was going broke! Pretty soon he would have to start taxing his people. He shuddered at the thought.

I can hold out for another month or so, he thought. *Especially if I move into a smaller place. This castle costs a lot to keep up. Maybe my next customer will have a high-priced problem.*

Then a visitor was announced.

"Your Highness, this young man seeks to hear any advice you may have about happiness."

Good, the king thought. *Another customer for happiness advice.*

"Step up here, lad," said the king, almost greedily. "What is your problem?"

The young man seemed terribly sad. From his expensive clothes, the king predicted a very high price *for his advice. But what if I can't help him? he thought. Even the king had lost faith in himself by this time.*

"Have you guessed the ending already, Todd? These fairy tales are all very much alike, aren't they? You haven't? Okay then, I'll finish the story."

The young man said, "Great King, your wisdom has let my father prosper. He has earned riches not possible in other kingdoms. But can your wisdom help me? Though I have everything and though I try to be happy, I am still unhappy. I laugh out loud to myself, smile in the mirror, buy new clothes and horses and jewels every day. But still I am not happy." And he cried right in front of the Great King.

The king smiled to himself. "This will be easy money," he thought. "I'll just give him my usual happiness advice."

"I will help you," the king said. "But first, do you swear by the happiness I will show you how to find that you'll never repeat the words I shall now tell you?"

"Yes, Great King. I do so swear."

The king went on. "And are you prepared to pay the high price for such advice?"

"Yes, Great King, I have a golden ring worth hundreds of goats."

So the king drew a small card from his royal robe with the happiness advice neatly written on it. (You see, the king never said the words aloud for fear that some spy would overhear. After all, his advice was a trade secret.)

The words on the card made the young man smile a real smile for the first time in his long, sad life. The words were:

> Having things is something but not
>   everything.
> Earning the values for your life is more than
>   just something, it's everything!

"Remember those words, lad. Get to know and understand their meaning. Happiness is quite simple, you know. There's nothing in the world that you cannot face. Do not fear! Fear is the ugliest thing because it alone equals unhappiness."

The king's speech was finished, so he asked the young man for the golden ring.

"May I ask you a question first, Great King?"

"Yes, ask it!" said the king, a little impatiently.

"Why, Great King, should I have to pay for your advice if your own son couldn't be made happy by it? And what good is your advice? Why should I give you my most precious treasure—my golden ring?"

The Great King was silent for the first time. He had always had a wise answer, but now he said nothing.

"Let me tell you something, Great King. Let me give you some advice for a change. I think you need it. Why, you yourself are not happy. I can see it in

your face."

The young man reached into his robe, pulled out a card of his own and gave it to the king. The king turned pale when he saw it. It said:

Let your son practice what you preach!
Let your son discover the truth that I
   already know: "Having things is something but not everything.
Earning the values for your life is more than
   just something, it is everything!"
Let your prince earn the values for his
   own life!

The king said, "Maybe you're right, lad. I gave him too much. Just as your father has done to you. And if only I could find my son, I would try your advice. My wisdom tells me that you are right—that giving him too much was a great error.

"Find my son and bring him to me! If your advice helps him to find happiness, then you shall inherit the kingdom and all that I own."

"Your Highness, I have already found him. He knows my advice and now he is truly happy," said the young man.

The king was astounded at these words. And he knew their truth when he saw the golden ring—the one he'd given to his son, the prince.

The young man removed his disguise and said, "Yes, Father, I am he—your son and the rightful prince of this kingdom. I have earned happiness and the right to inherit all that is ours."

Needless to say, they lived happily ever after.

Lisa ended the story. Todd was trying to think it through. He didn't understand it completely yet.

The day had been a bright new beginning for Lisa. She forgot her sadness. She had made a real plan for the children of Grand Avenue. And she had, during the course of her fairy tale, found a grain of precious truth.

She was happy.

■

The Glenbard plan worked perfectly. On the night of January first, Grandville became a ghost town. Its citizens and their secret treasures disappeared from the face of the earth. Or so, at least, it seemed to the fearsome and cruel army of Chidester—and Elm.

CHAPTER ELEVEN

The move to Glenbard had been kept "top secret" until the very last minute. Only the militia captains knew about it.

The children were awakened that night by the captains, who had memorized their orders: "Don't be frightened. We're moving to a new home tonight. Get all of your stuff and bring it to the front of Jill's house. But quiet—not a sound!"

The children moved quietly and obediently. They were standing patiently by the truck in less than half an hour.

After forming two lines, they passed their possessions into the truck from both sides. After the truck bottom was filled, the children scrambled up to sit on top of the bags and backpacks. The truck carried them to the fortress in the darkness.

At Glenbard, two human chains formed again. The

children lifted their belongings out of the truck and into the safety of the building.

In the pitch black of the school basement, they were told to remain quiet and to listen. Lisa spoke to them. "It's very important that you know some absolute rules. This is my city, Glenbard. We can all live here in safety, but we can't make one single mistake. You must follow every rule, or you'll be asked to leave. If you don't like the rules, then you are free to move back to your homes. You don't have to stay here.

"The Chidester Gang and others will be looking for us and for our treasures. We can't give them the slightest clue that we are here. For the next two weeks, we're going to work hard to make the city into a fortress. It will be like a castle, and we must build it quietly. From the outside, this building will look and sound completely deserted.

"Okay, here are the rules for the next two weeks. Listen carefully! There will be no candles or lights at any time. You must not leave the building except at night and then only if you're going out on a special mission. Don't go near windows or any place where they can see you from outside. You must never, ever shout. Always talk softly or whisper.

"If you are building or doing any project that is noisy, you must do it in the basement furnace room. We will explain the daily schedule later when we show you around. Just be prepared for two weeks of the hardest work you've ever known. There will be no playing, no noise, no mistakes, until we're finished.

"Then," she said, as if to give them courage, "when it's

finished, we'll announce the new city to the world. We'll make a lot of noise, and we'll celebrate."

The children were quiet for the rest of the night. Only a few muffled questions broke the silence.

■

Morning came, and sunlight filled their new home. The children wandered around, looking at the many curious sights. Someone had been busy in Glenbard, changing the old school into the place where they now lived.

At nine, Lisa and Jill took the citizens on a tour of their new city. They would live in the upper west section, facing Lake Ellyn. The classrooms had been converted into small apartments, with mattresses on the floor and blinds over the windows. Each apartment had a wash table in one corner with a pail of water, a metal pan, soap, towels, and a large mirror. A family name was written on each door.

Jill and Lisa had assigned the rooms, dividing all the children into "families." Jill's adopted children were organized into four groups of four roommates. Jill had a room with her own sisters, Katy and Missy.

The building could eventually hold four or five hundred citizens, maybe even more. But now there were only 35 kids who seemed to disappear in the huge place. As they toured the indoor city, Jill and Lisa took turns explaining their plan.

"This will be our cafeteria," Lisa was saying. "We'll

eat our meals at eleven and five each day. Don't be late or you'll go hungry. Julie and Nancy, will you take charge of the cooking?" They agreed.

Lisa made it clear that everyone would have a specific job in the city. There would be weekly meetings to discuss any job changes.

She told them that Glenbard was now her private property and that they were all welcome to stay. But she wanted everyone to do something to support the city. She wanted and needed them with her. But they had to know the rules.

Lisa went on. "Someday soon, we hope to have many other children here with us, and that will make it easier. For a while, though, it will be very hard work. At least we'll be safe."

"Here is our hospital," said Jill, as they passed the old Glenbard nurse's office. "I'm in charge of it. Missy and Katy will be my nurses. Be sure you come to me if you have even the tiniest pain. We have lots of medicine, and I'm studying books about first aid and those things. I will become a real doctor as fast as I can."

The children peered into the small, white room. It had two small beds with bright, clean sheets. There were cabinets of books and, in the corner by the window, there was a big sink and some odd-looking metal equipment.

They moved along to a group of three classrooms.

"Here is where you'll come to school," Jill said. "For a while, there will be no weekends in our city. It sounds awful, but we have a lot to learn and no time to waste.

There will be holidays for those who study and work hard."

They all sat down in one of the classrooms. Lisa said, "You must report to class at seven in the morning. We'll have juice and crackers, so you won't get too hungry. We'll stop for chores and lunch from ten until noon. Then we'll have classes again from noon until two. After that, we'll work on building Glenbard into a real city.

"Craig will be in charge of the school, but Jill and I will teach some classes too. We'd like Julie Miller and her roommates to be teachers' assistants during the work periods. Okay, girls?" It was. Lisa motioned for Craig to take over.

He didn't like to speak in front of large groups, but he was excited about his new job as a teacher. This is almost as good as having that farm, he thought to himself. And it's sure better than being the militia general.

"In the morning," he began, "we'll all attend survival classes—Lisa, Jill, and I will teach them. You'll learn about cooking, first aid, basic farming, camping, and so on. Jill will teach the youngest of you, so if you're under five, you must meet with Jill here in this room. All children older than five will meet with Lisa and me in classroom number three.

"Now, in the afternoon, we'll have special advanced classes. I know it sounds funny, but we all have to start planning for our full-time jobs. We're teaching farming, medicine, defense, machinery, and building. Other courses will be added later.

"Everyone must choose a job in one of these areas.

Your morning teacher will help you decide. The afternoon classes won't begin for a month, so you'll have time to make up your mind. Any questions?" There were none, and Craig sat down.

"Oh, yes," he remembered, "during this week everyone must report to the strategy room after lunch. We've got a lot of planning to do—especially in defense."

"What is a strategy room?" asked Katy.

"Come along and we'll show you," said Jill.

It was a strange-looking room with a lot of blackboards and maps of Glen Ellyn. On the far wall were photos and drawings of Glenbard and the land around it. On the long table, there was a plan of the school that showed the rooms and halls. There were about 40 toy soldiers sitting on the table.

Charlie was the new militia general.

"Strategy," Charlie said, "means planning. In this room, we will pretend in advance how battles might go so that we'll be ready to fight them. See these play soldiers on the table? Now, we can pretend that the enemy has entered the building at this door over here." He pointed to a place on the drawing. "We'll put these toy soldiers here to stand for the enemy. To plan our strategy, we can move our soldiers to different places on the drawing and decide the best way to handle this particular situation. By using the maps, blackboards, and other things, we can practice hundreds of different strategies."

Charlie added, "Todd Nelson, Steve Cole, Kevin, and his three roommates will be my captains. Is that all perfectly clear?" He asked the question in a sharp, military tone. It sounded like something he'd learned while watching a war movie.

They all understood. Katy said, "That sounds like a fun game. Can I play it too, sometime?"

"War is not a game!" replied the tough new general.

Jill and Lisa led them from the strategy room to the library. "This library has books mainly for older kids, so we're going to take the truck to the Glen Ellyn library and move their books over here. Eventually, we'll have six rooms of library space.

"After the city is built, we can have candles after dark. Then you can come here to read during the evening."

Next, they showed them the game room, which didn't look much like a game room yet. There were just a few toys, but Jill and Lisa promised to fill the room by the time Glenbard was finished.

There were many other rooms. Three rooms next to the cafeteria were for storing food, and two just down the hall were for supplies. There was a special room with huge wooden bars and several padlocks. "Here's where we'll store our guns and bombs and things like that," said Jill.

Later they would prepare other rooms: the automobile shop for fixing cars, the woodworking classroom for building things, and the home economics room for cooking classes.

There were many more plans for the city. But for now, their lives would be simple. Defense and food supplies were their biggest problems. These must be taken care of before anything else.

Julie and Nancy made the first morning meal at Glenbard out of soup and powdered milk. After lunch, Lisa, Jill, and Craig organized the others into work groups. There was a lot to be done, and no time to waste.

Lisa and Jill had done a good job of preparation. Everyone could see that they had already put in many late-night hours of hard work. The city already seemed like a cozy place.

By six, the Glenbard citizens had sore muscles and feet, but they were also excited and happy about their new home. Lisa could hear it in their playful whispers. "Quiet down now . . . get to sleep . . . no candles!" She made an inspection of the family rooms.

That night, Lisa had a private talk with each of the family leaders. "Do you understand the rules? Our lives depend on total quiet and secrecy. I am trusting you to take charge of this room. Come to me the minute something, even the slightest thing, seems wrong. Make sure that no one moves from their beds until I come by again in the morning."

From outside, Glenbard was still a deserted old high-school building. There were no signs of life.

But there *was* a light—a secret light—in Glenbard. A small candle burned in a tower room that had been carefully sealed. Wooden panels covered the window and the door to the hall. The edges of the panels were taped shut with black tape. From the outside, the room was as lightless as a coffin.

The secret room was for Glenbard's council. The

chamber would glow inside for many, many nights to come. It was here, in endless meetings, that the leaders would shape the future of the city. The candle's light painted shadows across their faces as they sat whispering around the small table.

Lisa was in charge of these conferences. Tonight they were discussing the old problem of making a defense plan. None of them liked to talk about it, but it had to be done. And the new plan had to be good.

Looking at her notes, Lisa made her defense proposal. "The way I see it, the first thing to do is to seal this place up so that no one could possibly get in. I'm talking about steel and bolts, not wood and nails. We should put solid steel covers over the inside of every door and window. I noticed that all the doors in the gym and bathrooms are made of metal. We can use them."

"Hey, I know," said Craig. "In the auto shop classroom, there's some welding equipment. My Uncle Elliot was a welder. I don't think you need electricity to work it. You just light the end of the torch and gas comes from the tank. There are lots of tanks down there." It didn't make sense to Lisa right away.

"What do you mean?" she asked.

"Well, we could weld the metal doors to the steel window frames. Nothing is stronger than welding!" he explained.

"What's wrong with bars?" asked Jill. "It will be awfully dark in here if the windows are all covered over. I wouldn't like that."

"It's not what we like that counts right now," Craig

said. "Anyway, with bars someone could throw firebombs inside or spy on us."

"It sounds all right to me," said Lisa. She thought for a moment. "But just think of the work it would take. There must be a thousand windows in this place." She thought again. "Why not just the first floor for now? Then Jill can have her light up here. Our other defenses, I think, will take care of the upper stories. We don't want any changes to be seen from the outside till the very last minute. Craig, can you get it all set up first—everything cut and fitted and ready to go so we can put them all up on the last night?"

"I think I can," he said.

"Well, check it out and report to us tomorrow night."

Their plans were very detailed. They tried to consider every possibility and take no chances. The mistakes of Grandville were mentioned. This time they wanted to be sure.

They spent hours and hours plotting defense. On many nights they talked until daylight. The room quickly filled up with candy wrappers, piles of notes and drawings, and empty soda cans that covered the table and the floor. It was an odd feeling for them to walk out of the dark and messy chamber into the bright sunlight of the hall.

The defense plan was taking shape. "Napoleon himself could learn from it," Craig boasted one night.

They would dig a secret tunnel entrance from the bushes and then through the hill on Lake Road. Charlie's dogs would be an important part of the plan. "You'd better give us a progress report soon. Let's keep the dogs away from here till they're trained. We can collect them at the airport, maybe in a hangar," said Lisa. She could easily imagine the dogs barking all night and giving them away.

But the roof defense was the main part of the plan. There'd be a dozen sentries on duty at all times. Dressed in black, and wearing black masks, they'd each patrol about 200 feet of roof line. A small storage shed near each sentry's station would hold guns, ammunition, and a hundred Molotov cocktails.

The brick-wall rim of the flat roof was a perfect shield. There were spaces in the rim for guns to rest on, just like the ramparts of a real castle. The rim was high enough to protect the sentries. Only their heads would show above it. The top of the barrier would be lined with bricks, glass fragments, and paper bags of sand. During an attack, the sentry could run on a board along the edge and shower the enemy with missiles.

The children invented a very dangerous weapon for serious attacks. They put drums of oil next to each sentry shed. These could be heated over wood fires, and pails of the boiling oil could be poured over the rim of the roof onto any enemies brave enough to scale the walls.

At half-hour intervals during the night, each sentry would drop a stone to the ground from his station. If the dogs stirred or barked at the sound, the sentry would know that all was well and that the guardians below were alert and ready.

All these plans made up just a small part of Glenbard's total defenses. After the Glenbard flag was raised and the city was ready, nothing would harm them. There would be no need for face-to-face fighting. The children could defend their home without going over the wall. All they had to do was keep watch and, if necessary, drop things on their attackers.

In the night, the citizens of Glenbard slipped silently from the fortress and went to all the hidden parts of Glen Ellyn, loading, looting, training, and even spying. They moved about in silence.

After the first week, the old high school still seemed deserted. Where are the children of Grand Avenue? old friends and enemies wondered.

At the same time, things were changing mysteriously around town. It was puzzling to the other children. "Hey, where did that big pile of sand go?" they'd ask one another. "It was in front of the lumber yard yesterday." Or, "Look! Someone's been in the library . . . the shelves are almost empty." Or, "I thought I heard someone outside the house last night, and then I heard dogs barking. It was scary. It sounded like a hundred dogs barking all at once."

The night council meetings continued. "We'll never have it ready on schedule," Lisa complained one night, in the second week of their work. "Charlie, how's your dog training coming along?"

"Okay, I guess, but I haven't been able to work at it for four days," he explained. "When there's snow on the roads, we can't go out. Our tracks will lead the enemy right to our door."

"Good thinking," Lisa complimented him. "I'm sure

glad you thought of that! Don't take any chances. We just can't make any dumb mistakes.

"Okay," she continued, bringing the meeting to a new topic. "I want to talk about an idea that I had last night. There is safety in numbers, and we haven't come close to filling this place up. We just rattle around. There's too much work to do and too few kids to do it. Besides, it would be much safer if people were living in all parts of the building."

"Get to the point, Lisa," said Craig. He was tired. It had been a long day.

She glared at him for a moment. "It's just that I haven't thought it through very well. But I think we should fill Glenbard with people. I want to rent parts of our fortress to other kids."

"Uh-oh, here she goes again," said Craig to Jill. "I can't take this. I'm going to bed."

"Stay where you are. It's important," Lisa said. Jill was silent.

"You see, we've got something special here. Safety— and many things that other kids don't have, like the library, the gym, and the supplies.

"After Glenbard is finished, we can go around Glen Ellyn telling kids about the nice life they could have here. If they can follow our rules and do their share of the work, we could let them join us. They'll pay us with their work."

"Yes," said Jill. "I think you're right. In fact, I'm sure you're right. Just think of how much easier things would be. Julie and Nancy would have help with the cooking.

And we'd have more friends, more new ideas . . . and fewer possible enemies, because they'd be in with us, instead of out there joining gangs."

"But that's the problem," Craig said, still in his bad mood. "When we start adding people, they'll bring new problems with them. How many of them will be spies? How many arguments will we have about rules and things? Suppose some group of kids decides to take over? And don't forget, more people eat more food."

He was right about the spy danger, and Lisa knew it. But she defended her idea. "I've thought a lot about those problems and I'm sure we can solve them. First, we'll have a list of rules for the new people, and they'll have to sign an agreement, like a contract."

"I think we should just take families we know personally," said Jill "That way we'd be safer. I can think of at least a dozen families I know of that we could trust, and so could every other kid.

"How many people do you think we should plan for, Lisa?" Jill asked.

"Well," she answered carefully, "I think we should start really small, just to see what problems come up. Let's say, for example, that we took in three families to start with—no more than a dozen new kids altogether. That would give my plan a good test, and we could grow from there."

Craig seemed encouraged by the idea. His harsh look faded.

Lisa went on. "I have been studying the floor plan of Glenbard, and it seems to me that we might eventually have a city of about 800."

Craig got up and left the room. "Eight hundred," he muttered to himself. "Eight hundred!" He felt like swearing out loud.

"He's really mad, Lisa." Jill started after him.

"Wait, Jill. Let him go. I'll talk to him when he cools off a little. Something else is bothering him, I can tell. He's been acting strange. I hate to say it, but I don't think he likes it here. He's probably got the farm on his mind again!"

The two girls talked about Lisa's new idea in detail. It seemed to have endless possibilities. "As soon as the city is finished, we'll go out and talk to some families," Jill said. "We'll each find one. Three families will make a good test."

"Yes, but let's not talk about it with Craig much. We'll wait and let him get interested on his own. Maybe he'll see that it would mean more students for his school and more teachers, too. And even more farmers, for that matter."

The two girls stared at the candle for some time, thinking about the new plan. Finally Jill spoke, changing the subject.

"Lisa, why do you keep calling it *your* city—saying that it's *your* property?"

"Because it is! I thought I told everyone that on the very first day."

"But we've all helped to build it, haven't we?" argued Jill. "The kids are starting to call you selfish. They don't like it when you call it yours. They want to own it too."

"Selfish? I guess I am. But there's more to it than that. Don't forget, it was *my* discovery. The place was just sitting here empty, belonging to no one. I found it, I planned it, I filled it with *my* supplies, and now I run it.

"Nobody else seems to want my job, you know. Craig will probably wind up going off to *his* farm. And you'll leave too, someday, and start *your* hospital. Will it be selfish for him to own his own farm? Will people call him selfish for selling the crops from *his* farm?

"Why should this be any different? At first, I didn't think it made any difference at all, but then I started to imagine what would happen to Glenbard if more than one person was in charge. If a city belonged to no one in particular, it wouldn't get anywhere!

"No, Jill. I know that you like to share things, but it just doesn't work out the way you'd like it to. In the first place, nothing would ever get done. With no one in charge and no one to make decisions, the group would argue all the time about whose property should be shared. And then everybody would be squabbling about how to divide things up, and they'd be too busy to accomplish anything.

"I do own this place, and I don't force anyone to stay. I didn't force you or anyone else to come here. It's a free thing. I'm willing to take the worries and the responsibility, but I'll keep control, thanks.

"Call me selfish all you like, but I don't want to *own* anybody. I don't want anyone to *own* me, and that's what a sharing group wants to do."

Jill didn't feel like arguing. "Well, anyway," she said, "I think you're in for trouble if you keep calling it *your* city."

Lisa considered her next words carefully. "Freedom is more important than sharing, Jill. This is my city. I plan to run it well and build it into something good. But I have to do it the way I think is best."

Jill left Lisa alone in the tower chamber. Jill was angry, like Craig, though her thoughts about Lisa weren't as critical as his. She sure is stubborn, thought Jill. I hope she doesn't regret it!

Lisa's thoughts were more harsh. I'm not being very smart, she told herself. I need their help, and it's dumb to make them angry. I suppose I can talk more about *our* city, if that will make them happy. But I can't lose control. If I'm ever going to rebuild things, it's got to start with this city. To fill Glenbard with more people would be good for every one of us. It would make life safer and easier.

But she also began to see her job more clearly. She would have to work hard to *earn* her goals. She'd have to offer something better to the children than they could find anywhere else. Like in the kingdom of Real Fun, she thought, smiling.

Lisa didn't sleep that night, except for brief moments in front of the candle, when her head rested on her crossed arms.

■

On the night of January 16, the ghostly old school

building came mysteriously to life. Lights filled the upstairs windows, and there was joyous shouting and excitement on the roof. The glow of a dozen torches dotted the roof line. Horns blared, and a hundred dogs below barked as if to drown out the sounds above them. To the silent audience below, Glenbard looked like a castle.

Cherry bombs burst as they fell from the rim of the roof. Bottle rockets were shot at the moon and then fell to the lake below.

The children on the rooftop said that this celebration was even better than the first holiday in Grandville. There was a lot more to celebrate. The blistered hands that clapped and touched other hands had built something new.

The children on the outside, watching from dozens of dark places, finally had the answer to their mystery. They knew where Grand Avenue had gone. The strange night happenings of the past weeks at last made sense.

If those watching children had been able to stand in the cold throughout the night, they would have learned even more. The celebration lasted till dawn. The citizens of Glenbard sang a new song, and they shouted cheers and challenges that broke the silence of the icy night.

At sunrise, an awkward, small bugler sounded a new call. Slowly, a bright orange-and-yellow flag was raised above the new city.

CHAPTER TWELVE

The next year was a busy, happy time at Glenbard. Word of the new city spread quickly. Every day, children called up from the street to a rooftop sentry, "Can we join your city?" A committee of three would emerge from a heavy door under the protection of the rooftop sentries. The committee would ask: "Who are you? Where did you live? Why did you leave? What gang did you join? Who was the leader? Why did you quit?" All of these questions and several more had to be answered.

Many were turned away—not for lack of room, but because no one in the city knew them or because someone in the city *did* know them and said they couldn't be trusted. The committee wouldn't take any chances. Craig was the most skeptical of the three. He asked hard, tricky questions like, "Do you know my good friend, Tom Logan?" The unwise child who thought any friend of Tom Logan could get in had to leave.

But many new families were taken in, and the city changed. There were crowds of new citizens who brought their own ideas. By summer there were 90 kids at Glenbard. By September, the classrooms had over 300 students. The population kept growing.

On January 16th of the next year, almost 400 citizens jammed the rooftop for the evening celebration. They shouted challenges to the armies who threatened them from below. By the end of April, 19 months after the plague, Glenbard's population was just over 500.

Some of them thought that the girl who owned the city was very odd. "How could a girl own a city?" they said. "Why *should* a girl own a city? People don't *own* things like cities!"

Others just disliked her. "What does she do for Glenbard?" they asked. "We hardly ever see her." But they knew that she was not idle. It was rumored that she only slept every other night, and that she still worked by candlelight in the dark tower chamber. "What a silly thing!" they said. "There's no need for that anymore."

During the day, however, Lisa did make her presence felt. She inspected the kitchen, gave orders to workers who were getting new rooms ready, sent her trucks to secret supply places, and settled arguments between the citizens.

Most of the children admired her and liked her strong way of doing things. She always seemed busy, and though she did not smile or laugh very often, they could tell by the way she moved about that she was happy. "You'd be happy, too, if you owned a whole city," someone said.

But Lisa was finding that it wasn't easy running a city, especially one growing as fast as hers. There were problems every minute of the day. "Lisa, we're out of fuel for the torches," Charlie might tell her. She would answer, "Well, I'll add it to the supply list. It will be here by tonight. How much do you need?"

Then there were not enough books. "Go get them from the Lombard schools," she'd decide. There was a big fight in the west wing. "Bring them to me." Room 110 wouldn't be ready by tomorrow, and the Wilson kids were getting tired of living in the gym. "Well, get somebody to work through the night. We promised to have it ready!"

The leaders of the city always seemed to be one step behind the problems. Still, it was exciting. They had great fun at their meetings, laughing at the funny things that happened each day. They teased each other but grew to be friends.

"You're not going to believe what Lisa did today," said the construction manager. "She gave us drawings for the family rooms in the south basement area and forgot to put any doors in three of the apartments."

"This place is all confusion. You know what it's like to build walls without nails? Not easy. But it's even harder without wood! When can we get some lumber?"

There were lots of problems, but the council had plenty of help. The new children brought new skills to

Glenbard. They were all happy to be free of gangs and starvation. For many months, the problems seemed challenging and exciting.

"Planning is the secret," Lisa said over and over again. "If we can anticipate problems before they happen, then we'll succeed." They had never run a city before, and they learned most of their lessons the hard way. But they seemed to be making enough right decisions. Things were going well. Soon Glenbard would be full.

"Not bad for a year's work!" Lisa boasted. And then she admitted what was also true. "A year of very hard work," she said, as she studied the tired faces of her assistants—Craig, Jill, Steve, Todd, Charlie, and the six new council members.

Glenbard's defense plan was the biggest success of all. There had been eight enemy attacks and none of them had lasted more than 10 minutes. Boiling oil in the face had a way of making a gang leader choose other targets.

There had been attacks by seven different gangs. Six never tried a second time. But Tom Logan tried twice. He dreamed up a clever plan for the second attack, but it wasn't clever enough to beat the rooftop soldiers, who scarred his face with the burning oil. Charlie wondered if revenge would bring Tom back a third time with his 150 soldiers.

Charlie was turning out to be a good military leader, but he was worried about Logan. "Lisa," he said at one council meeting. "I think he's going to be back. Tom's no dummy. We've got to watch out for him. For some reason he wants to get us."

"Charlie, you worry too much," she said. Looking at Craig, she added, "You generals are all alike!"

They both looked back at her. Craig said, "Lisa, you don't worry enough!"

Later that night, alone in the tower chamber, Lisa thought about what Craig had said. Maybe he had a point. They couldn't take any chances. Logan could have spies in Glenbard already, and even if Tom gave up, there were plenty of other gangs. The city had to be prepared.

She'd discuss it with Charlie tomorrow. They would figure out some new plan. Maybe a walking army of their own was what they needed. After all, they had 510 people—or was it 518? She couldn't even keep track anymore.

They wonder why I seem so strong. They think I'm something special because I run my own city. Don't they see that it's fun, and that any one of them could do it, too? All you have to do is look at the old world for the clues. There are hundreds of books that tell you how to do it.

Then, in a harsher tone, she said out loud, "You know the truth, don't you? You're still a kid just like the rest of them. How did you get yourself into all of this? You're scared to death, aren't you? And tired, too." She tried to think of tomorrow's problems. It didn't work.

The citizens wondered why she sat in this dark room. They called it her 'chamber.' But she couldn't leave the room or change it in any way. It was the only place where she could really think.

Then thinking became too hard, and she decided to inspect the roof sentries. She went outside. The fresh air felt good. It cleared her mind.

"How does it look tonight, Jody?" She was glad she had remembered the sentry's name.

"Looks just fine, Lisa. But you'd better tell Charlie to do something about those dogs. I dropped my stone a few minutes ago and there was no barking at all. They must all be sleeping. Maybe we've been feeding them too much." When he turned again to look at her, she was peering over the wall.

"Jody! Come here and look. The dogs *do* seem to be sleeping—but it's not right. You can't feed them *that* much food. There's something wrong! Something is wrong!

"Sound the 'quiet' alarm and get the militia up here. Now!" she ordered. While he passed the word, she ran to the other end of the building. All the dogs were lying still.

"I'm going down to see what's the matter," she called to the nearest sentry. "Get some kids with rifles over here to cover me. Here, help me with the rope ladder. Todd, is that you?" She had forgotten that her little brother had sentry duty on the rooftop this night.

On the way down she realized her mistake. If there was trouble, why was she going down into it? But it was too late—she was on the ground.

She went to the nearest dog. Its body was cold. She ran to the next. Dead. She knew they had been poisoned.

She started to run for the rope ladder, but her path was blocked by a boy with a hideous scar on his face.

"Let me by!" she ordered, but he was not from Glenbard, and he grabbed her.

She bit him until he screamed. Two soldiers rushed to his rescue and grabbed her by the arms. She couldn't move.

"Let me go! Sentry!" she shouted to the roof. "Pull the ladder up, quickly!"

"Lisa," the boy with the scarred face said, "it won't help for you to fight. I've got 200 soldiers surrounding your lousy Glenbard. It was nice of you to drop in," he laughed. "Don't you recognize me with my new face? I'm Tom Logan. Your boiling oil trick won't work tonight, Lisa. Your city is not your city anymore. It's *ours* now. So relax. I don't want to hurt you." For a moment he seemed almost kind.

But she didn't believe him. She fought him and, somehow, she broke free and ran. "Stop, Lisa, or we'll shoot! Stop, Lisa! We don't want to . . . ."

Those were the last words she heard. There was a deadly pain in her, somewhere, and she fell silently near the bushes.

"Who did that?" Logan shouted. "I told you not to shoot until I gave the order. See if she's all right!"

A soldier studied her body and came back to Tom with his report. "I think she's dead. There's blood all over her head, and she isn't breathing."

Tom shuddered. In all his violent days, he had never killed anyone. He knew it was a mistake, but did that really change anything? Why her? he wondered for a moment.

"Don't shoot till I say so!" he shouted. Tom then shouted a bluff to the sentry above. "We've got her! We've got your leader! So don't throw any of your junk down here or we'll kill her. And I mean it! Open the big door—we're coming in!" The doors opened slowly.

The army of Chidester, Elm, and Lenox streets filed into Glenbard. They took over the city without resistance. They had the guns and the girl who owned the city.

"You see!" boasted Tom Logan to his captains. "I *knew* it would work. Wasn't I right?" Now *he* was the leader of the city.

Tom's soldiers were everywhere. The citizens of Glenbard were frightened and helpless. Their lives had changed into a nightmare.

"Where is Lisa?" Craig demanded.

Tom bluffed again. "We're keeping her below in a safe place, just to be sure you don't do something stupid. We'll kill her if you try anything dumb!"

Tom turned to Craig. "You're the next-in-command, aren't you? Well, go tell your loyal citizens that their home sweet home is under new ownership. Go ahead, tell them! And while you're at it, tell them not to try anything dumb. Remember, we've got Lisa!"

Craig had no choice. He turned Glenbard over to Logan without a fight. The girl who built the city was suddenly powerless—a captive, or worse.

PART THREE

FEAR IS WHAT YOU FEEL WHEN
YOU WAIT FOR SOMETHING
BAD TO HAPPEN . . .

AND FUN IS WHAT YOU HAVE
WHEN YOU FIGURE OUT A WAY TO
MAKE SOMETHING GOOD HAPPEN.

CHAPTER THIRTEEN

Todd watched the encounter from the top of the wall. When he saw Lisa fall near the bushes, he dropped to the roof and began sobbing. While the others met Tom Logan downstairs, no one noticed the little boy crying in the darkness.

After a time, his tears dried, and he began to think. Was she really dead? How could he know for sure? He had to find out for himself. She can't be dead, he decided, as he climbed down the rope ladder.

But when he came near her, it seemed that he was wrong. He fell upon her body in tears. "No!" he cried out loud. He couldn't believe it. For a long time he rested his head on her chest.

He noticed something and suddenly raised his head. "She's breathing. She's breathing! Lisa, *Lisa!*" He whispered it, frightened that some enemy would hear.

"She's okay. She's alive!" Somehow he had to get help. He knew that the enemy was everywhere inside Glenbard and that soon they would assign roof guards. He climbed back up the wall and moved the rope ladder to a spot directly above Craig's window. He lowered himself, slowly.

The window was locked. Craig was gone, but Erika was there, sleeping in her bed. Todd knocked on the window. As Erika turned and saw him hanging there, he put his finger to his lips. Cautiously, she came to open the window.

"What are you doing out there, Todd?"

"Don't you know what's happened? They've shot Lisa and taken over our city. Haven't you heard?"

"Oh, no!" she cried. "I didn't know, Todd. Is she hurt bad?"

"I think so. There's blood all over her, but she's still breathing." He still didn't know how bad Lisa was. "I can't come inside, Erika, so you have to help me. Can you pretend that you're sick . . . uh . . . with a stomachache?"

She didn't understand. He continued: "Try to look real sick, and go find Jill. Get her to take you to the hospital room. Tell her your stomach hurts. And find Craig. Have him come with you and Jill. If Tom Logan thinks you're sick, he'll leave you alone in the hospital room. I'll be waiting outside the window with a ladder. We have to take Lisa away, and I need help.

"Pretend like you want to throw up. Try it now so I can see." She looked awful. "That should work," he said.

"Be careful, Erika, and hurry. Please hurry."

Todd climbed back to the roof and walked along the rim to a point above the nurse's room. But he wasn't sure which window it was. Was it two windows over from the chamber tower or was it three? He couldn't remember. I'll have to take a chance, he thought, and climbed down.

Where are they? he wondered, looking into the spotless room. He thought about his sister. What could have gone wrong? Suddenly the door opened, and four people entered the room. Todd pulled away from the glass. He had the right room, it seemed. Logan was with them and stayed for a long time, arguing with Craig.

Todd peeked in now and then at the edge of the window. Erika looked awful, like she would actually throw up. Logan told a guard to watch the hall and then closed the door behind him.

They opened the window, and Jill whispered, "Where is she hurt? What should I bring? The stretcher? Throw it down to the ground, Craig. Can she talk? Here, take these bandages and get some alcohol . . . and . . . oh, what else will we need?"

They rounded up more supplies, just in case. "That should be enough," Jill said. "Let's go quickly. Erika, you'd better come with us."

Todd was the last one down. When he shut the window, the latch fell into place, locking the window from the inside. Figure that one out, Logan, Todd said to himself. When the three of them reached the ground, they ran. Craig carried the stretcher.

"All the dogs are sleeping, Toddy!" Erika hollered.

"Shut up," Todd said, not caring that the dogs were dead. They were quiet and maybe, because of it, Lisa could be saved. "Follow me." He led them to her body. "You help her, Jill. I'll get the car. Craig, you stand guard. Here's my gun. And, Erika," he added, "keep your mouth shut." Erika thought he was beginning to sound like his sister.

They slid the stretcher into the back seat. Lisa didn't move or even open her eyes, but she was still alive. Cold and silent, but alive. "How is she, Jill? Can you fix her up?" Todd started the car.

"Where are we taking her?" Craig asked.

When he heard the words "to the old farm on Swift Road," Craig was startled. After all this time, he thought, she's bringing me to the farm.

The beat-up old Cadillac carried the leaders away from Glenbard. The girl who owned a city was now without a home.

The old farm was quiet and undisturbed. "Look, Jill," said Craig. "There's an oil heater with its own fuel tank. All we need is a match."

The warmth—something they had learned to do without at Glenbard—would help make the operating room comfortable. Jill ran around, preparing the room and giving orders to Erika, Craig, and Todd.

Lisa was unconscious. They covered her with blankets and put her on a sofa. She stirred once and began to mumble. "What did she say?" asked Todd. Then she spoke again. "No chances, can't take any chan—"

"I wish she hadn't been on the ground for so long.

She's lost a lot of blood," said Jill. They covered Lisa with more blankets while Jill studied a first-aid book.

She was very nervous about the task that lay ahead of her. At Glenbard, she had treated cuts and injuries of all kinds, but she didn't have the faintest idea how to remove a bullet. There was nothing about it in the book. She threw it aside.

"Craig, tear this sheet into strips."

"How wide?" he asked.

"About six inches. Todd, try to find some whiskey in the kitchen. Erika, bring me some clean sheets, all you can find. No! No! Look in the linen closet—over there."

She would have to use the big dining-room table. "Todd and Craig, bring a mattress in here. There must be one in the bedroom . . . good . . . now go wash your hands."

"Jill, there's no water in the house," said Todd.

"Well, we've got to have water. Go find some quick. Get at least six full pails. Hurry! Go to the lake if you have to." Jill was getting panicky. Todd went out immediately. "Build a fire, Craig!"

Jill felt Lisa's forehead. "She's much cooler now than before. Where is that water? Did Todd actually drive to the lake? Maybe we could have collected rainwater."

Todd finally came back and put two pails of water on the fire to boil. "Okay," said Jill. "Who wants to be my assistant?" The Bergman children said they couldn't stand the sight of blood. "Todd, will you help?" He said he would.

"All right, scrub up. Wash like you've never washed before. We can't risk an infection. We can't take any chances." Then Jill was ready to begin. "Help me lift her up on the table."

Lisa looked very pale, and so did Jill and Todd. Jill undid the temporary bandage they had applied in the bushes. Lisa was still bleeding. Craig and Erika had to leave the room.

The sight of the wound would not have shocked nurses in a regular hospital. They might even have said that it was minor. But to Jill and Todd, it looked bad. Jill faced an awesome responsibility. Her life is in my hands, she thought. What if she dies? What do I do first?

"Todd, we've got to get that bullet out," Jill said. "Let's get started!" Her courage was returning.

"First, we have to wash away the dried blood. Bring warm water and strips of cloth." He went out of the room and quickly returned. "Now tear the strips into small pieces, about the size of washcloths. Are you sure your hands are clean? Here, pour some of this alcohol in a pan. We can dip our hands in it."

With warm water and soap, Jill dabbed away the dried blood. When it was clean, the wound didn't look bad at all. There was only a small hole in the arm where the bullet was lodged. "She must have fallen on her head," said Jill. "See the big bruise and cut by her eye? That's why there was so much blood on her face."

Now Todd understood why the Chidester soldier had pronounced Lisa dead. When he had seen all the blood on her face, he must have thought that it came from a bullet!

When Jill soaked the area around the wound with alcohol, she began to feel nervous again. So far it was fairly easy, but how was she going to get the bullet out? Should she cut a wider opening? Suppose she hit an artery?

She picked up the first-aid book and looked for the diagram of the circulatory system. She studied it over and over, looking from the page to Lisa's arm and then back to the page again.

"Oh, I get it now!" she shouted happily. "A small cut *this* way won't hurt anything. Todd, hold the blade of the razor in the flame for 30 seconds. That will sterilize it." Lisa stirred but said nothing. "It's a good thing she's still unconscious. I don't think she'd want to be awake for my first operation."

"Is she going to be all right?" Todd asked.

"Yes," Jill replied.

"Here goes." She was trembling, and she wanted to close her eyes. She made a shallow, two-inch cut. The bullet was lodged by the side of Lisa's arm bone, not far from the surface of the skin. Jill could feel it.

"Give me more pieces of cloth. No, better yet, keep dabbing the blood away, and I'll try to get the bullet out. Dab two or three times with each piece, then soak one in alcohol and dab just once. Keep that up. Always use a fresh piece of cloth."

Jill sterilized a pair of tweezers, then used them to reach into the opening and feel for the metal. "There it is," she said aloud. She slowly, carefully pulled out the bullet.

Tears were filling her eyes.

"Todd, I'm closing the wound. Get more alcohol, then we'll stitch it up. It won't be easy, but I think I know how."

"That wasn't too bad, was it?" she said, when they'd finished. "I think I'd make a good doctor."

■

In the middle of the night, Lisa woke up. Todd was sitting by her side. "Hi, Lisa," was all he said. She nodded to him. He could tell, as the drowsiness left her, that her arm hurt a lot. She groaned and turned away.

"Jill, come here!" Todd called. When she came into the room, he whispered, "I think something's wrong."

"Arm hurt?" asked Jill, not seeming very concerned. Lisa nodded again. "Well, it's supposed to hurt. We fixed you up just fine, but we had to do a little . . ." She started to tell the story of the surgery, but, fearing that she would alarm Lisa, she said instead, "We had to do a little work on your arm. It will feel better soon." As she left the room, she said, "I know just what you need."

She went to the kitchen and quickly returned. She handed Lisa a glass of golden-colored liquid. "Now drink it all, even if you don't like the taste," Jill said.

The drink looked much better than it tasted. Lisa took a big swallow and spit it out all over the blanket. "Now, Lisa," Jill teased. "Have you forgotten your manners?"

"Ick!" Lisa made a horrible face. "What was that stuff?"

"Whiskey," Jill answered, as if it were Kool-Aid.

"Are you trying to get me drunk? What kind of friend are you?" In spite of her pain, Lisa was teasing her.

"I'm serious, Lisa. Drink it all up. You'll need it for the pain, and you have to get some more rest." Jill handed her a full glass.

It took a long time for Lisa to finish but, for some reason, it got easier as the glass emptied. The last swallow was a big one. Lisa giggled. "Boy, do I feel funny."

Then Jill told Lisa what had happened. "Well," Lisa said, "sometimes one mistake is all it takes. I suppose if I could do a stupid thing like that, I deserved to lose the city. You've got to be smart to earn good things.

"And even that's not enough. You've got to be smart to keep them, too." After a long pause, she said, "I guess I'll just have to earn it all back. I'll figure something out."

The whiskey was making her dizzy. She started to giggle.

"I give up," Jill said. "You're drunk. Get some sleep. Call me if you need anything."

"That's okay," said Todd. "I'll be here to help her."

That night it was Todd who told a story. He started with a serious tale about a little prince in a faraway kingdom. But Lisa giggled in all the serious places. So he tried to change it into a funny, silly story. But he couldn't finish this one either. Soon, Lisa fell asleep.

Todd wasn't bothered. He knew his audience was at fault. He turned out the light and sank into the big chair. It was uncomfortable, so he decided to sleep on the operating table.

As he fell asleep, Todd thought about his sister. He was glad that she was better, because he was learning so much from her. Does she know that? he wondered.

■

The light in the Glenbard tower chamber burned through the night. A scarred face stared into the candle. Who shot her? Tom Logan wondered. I'll beat his little head in if I ever catch him.

He was angry, but not because he thought Lisa's death would make the citizens of Glenbard hate him or because it would make his job harder. He was mad because he hadn't wanted Lisa to get hurt. At least not that way. He was frustrated, too, for his luck, because that's all that this victory really was—a matter of luck. Most of all, he was mad at his own nameless fears.

CHAPTER FOURTEEN

Before dawn, the new leader of 700 sat thinking and planning how to manage his first day as leader of the city. He stared into the black void of the chamber, past the candle that had burned away. The candle, he thought. It was her candle and now the light is gone, and so is she.

■

The new leader of only four lay awake, thinking and planning how to bring back all that she had lost. She stared into the ever-brightening space of the window until sunlight poured into the room. Her body felt weak, but her mind was active. The city, she thought. It was my city, and now I've left it. I *must* go back!

Todd opened his eyes and stared at the strange ceiling until he recognized the lamp hanging above him. Last night the lamp was hanging ominously over his sister. Why had he slept there?

Then he remembered the night before. He quickly turned his head to study the patient. Her eyes were open, and they met his. She had been staring in his direction for some time.

"It's nice to wake up warm in the morning, isn't it, Todd? Maybe we can find more oil stoves and move them to Glenbard. Think of how cold it must be in the bedrooms. We should . . ." What had happened then came back to her. She fell silent.

Lisa and Todd each tried to construct a mental image of the distant city. What was it like now? Would they ever see it again? Of course they would! They both knew it.

She smiled and said, "Thanks for saving my life, Todd."

"How do you feel?"

"My arm hurts. Do you think you can find some aspirin for me?" He slipped down from the table and started rummaging through the nursing supplies.

Jill appeared at the doorway. "What you need is a glass of whiskey, Lisa."

"Are you kidding? Not a chance—that stuff is awful. I can still taste it from last night." She made a face and shook her head. "I'd rather suffer. Can't I have some aspirin?"

"Sorry, Lisa, but we forgot to bring it along," Jill said. "And this farm doesn't have any. In fact, the whole place is empty. Someone has been here already. But there's plenty of whiskey.

"Come on, Todd, get your coat. I'm starved. Maybe there will be supplies at the farmhouse across the road."

Jill and Todd left. The cheerful room was silent when Lisa suddenly remembered that she had already been to this farm. She had been the one, a long time ago, who had taken the food and even the aspirin. Now she remembered the old woman's note, her own wild idea about driving the car, the first ride, the chicken in the wicker basket, and the cookies in the jar. It seemed a long time ago.

Ever since she had awakened, she had felt an urgent need to recapture Glenbard. Now that need and her excitement helped her forget the pain in her arm. Aspirin or whiskey couldn't have done the job as well.

Lisa didn't doubt for a moment that they could save the city. But she also knew how strong Glenbard was. Winning back the city would take much more than confidence. How could four of them win against an army of hundreds?

How? . . . How? she asked a hundred times. And then the first seed of a plan began to grow. Ideas began streaming through her mind. Lisa didn't notice Jill and Todd come back through the door.

"Of course," she said out loud. "It will cost me plenty, but I can make a deal with another army. For two months worth of supplies, they'd help us capture the city. The dogs are gone, and that will help. And we know the city better than Logan. I wonder if anyone told him about the secret tunnel? If only we could get a spy inside."

She laughed to herself at the thought. A spy? Why,

we have hundreds of spies in there. She laughed again, and they turned to look at her. Was she delirious?

But her thinking had never been clearer. The ideas kept coming. Signals from a spy . . . a new plan of the city showing Logan's room . . . a hired army surrounding the city . . . disguises for the four of them . . . a daylight attack on the inside from the tunnel . . . a signal to the army on the outside . . .

"Lisa, do you want some breakfast?" somebody asked.

She didn't hear. Could they get to Logan without being detected? It should be a dawn attack. He's probably a late sleeper. A set of keys. We'll need that to get into his room. A small pistol . . .

"Her eyes are wide open, and her lips are moving a little," someone said.

That's it, she thought. *A gun to his stupid head. We'll hold him hostage till his army is out of the building, and then we'll lock him up for safekeeping. If we threaten to kill him, they'll leave us alone, at least till we can set up our defenses again.*

But . . . suppose the army doesn't need Logan anymore, and they decide to fight instead of walking out? They probably like it in there. I'll bet they've eaten up all the food. What if they fight us? Will they believe our threats about killing Logan? We have to take the chance. We'll signal our soldiers. They'll slip in through the tunnel, too. You can't see the entrance from the roof. Then when the Chidester Gang is gone, we can get back to work . . .

"Should I shake her, Jill?" Todd asked.

The battle was already fought and won in Lisa's mind.

When they're gone, we'll have to figure out a different kind of moat—one that's safer than a ring of dogs. We should find more cars with gas or find a way to get more gas. The parking lot is filling up with empty cars. What did I hear about portable electric generators? They run on gas, too, and we could get electricity from them. Just think of that! We'd have lights and stoves and refrigerators . . . and music . . . and computers . . .

She turned suddenly toward the breakfast table. "Music!" she shouted. "Music! Do you know that we haven't heard music in almost 19 months?"

They stared at her. The loud words startled them.

"Music, I said. Soon we'll have music at Glenbard." She couldn't understand their dumbfounded looks.

Now they were sure she was delirious. Jill walked over to the couch and stroked Lisa's forehead. "Relax a while, Lisa," she said. "Relax. We have food whenever you're hungry. Do you want a glass of water?"

Lisa understood. "Thanks, Jill. Really, I'm all right. I was just thinking about a plan to get the city back, and I guess I got carried away."

"Do you think you can walk to the table?" Jill asked. "We've made a nice breakfast. Yours may be a little cold by now, though."

Lisa tried to stand but fell back to the couch. Jill said, "You're weak, you know—you lost a lot of blood. Stay on the couch. I'll bring your food to you." The other children gathered by the couch to watch her eat.

"Eggs?" Lisa was amazed. "Where did you find this?"

While she ate the delicious cold egg, Todd explained.

"The farm across the road has a big supply of everything. We found a chicken in the bedroom. We couldn't figure out what she ate, but she had a nice bed and a nice house all to herself. That's how we found the egg."

"Smart chicken," Lisa said, with a smile. "I'll have to go meet our new neighbor and thank her for the breakfast. We must be neighborly and all that, you know!"

Craig continued the game. "I wonder if the old bird is afraid of chicken gangs?"

They each tried a joke about the chicken, and though the jokes got worse and worse, they laughed harder and harder. Everyone was feeling silly.

Finally, Jill stopped the fun with a serious question. "Lisa, what did you mean when you shouted the word 'music'? And why did you say we'd soon have music at Glenbard?"

Lisa told them about the electric generator and a little about the new strategy, but not all. She had to think it through more carefully. She found herself suddenly tired again. But there were a few things that they could get started on.

She looked at Todd for a moment and then said, "One of the things we need is a spy. We need someone to slip into Glenbard quietly, so Logan won't notice, and act like a regular citizen. Todd, will you do it?"

"Sure I will. No sweat!"

That made them laugh. Then Lisa turned to Jill. "Can you figure out a good disguise for Todd? He's going to be our spy. It has to be a perfect disguise. I'd hate to think of what they'd do to him if he were ever caught." Jill thought about it.

"Todd, you'll have to tell us how the place is set up now. You can pass messages to our friends inside."

"Sure, Lisa," he said.

"Okay, Todd should leave tonight. I'm tired now, and I feel like resting a little while. Let me know when the disguise is ready."

Lisa wanted to think more about the plan, but she was still very weak. While the sun warmed her body, she quickly fell asleep. The whole day passed while she lay on the couch. Plans drifted in and out of her dreams. Sometimes she was in a battle. At other times, she was in her chamber plotting out the future.

Jill and Todd tried many disguises. Most of them were hilarious. But none of them seemed to be real enough. They tried marking his face up with fake scars and parting his long hair down the middle. They used a package of hair dye from the neighboring farm. They laughed at the dark-haired Todd. But the disguise still wasn't good enough.

Craig spent most of his day out in the sun with Erika. They saw the bodies in the cattle barn. They saw the wonderful modern equipment in the huge garage—a new tractor, a corn picker, a set of plows. "With all this stuff, I guess it's a big farm," said Craig. "Eighty acres anyway." But he couldn't be sure from looking at the farmyard.

While Erika played in the empty chicken coop, Craig went inside to investigate the old farmer's study. He touched every book and thumbed through many of them. He sure knew what he was doing, Craig thought to himself. Just look at all his records. It'd be no sweat to get it going again!

He searched through all the drawers of the desk until he found what he wanted—a big ring of keys. He picked them up and ran out of the study. He tiptoed past Lisa's sleeping figure, slipped out the door, and ran at full speed to the equipment garage. Was he afraid to let her know what he was thinking? He would tell her about it later.

All he could think of now was the tractor. "Come on, Erika!" he ordered. "Hop up on the seat with me. Sure there's room. We'll make room. We're going to take a tour of our new farm.

"It's almost spring. No, it is spring! It's the middle of May. Pretty soon we'll be planting our crops. You're a big girl now, Erika. Do you think you can run the house and learn to cook? If I can learn to farm, you can learn to cook!"

While they talked, Craig fumbled with the gear shift on the tractor. He pushed and tugged and wished he could swear. Maybe that *wasn't* the shift lever. He tried every other stick or button he could reach. No . . . nothing. Finally, he gave up and said, "I'll figure it out later. Come on, Erika, we'll just have to walk around our farm."

The walk took several hours. It was a much larger farm than he'd imagined. By the time the tired children returned to the farmhouse, they had seen every hill, every fence, and every inch of ground on the place. They knew they would like their new home.

Erika laughed at what she saw inside. So did Craig. The laughter pulled Lisa out of her long dream. She turned her head toward the happy sounds and blinked her eyes in disbelief.

There was a stranger in the house. "Who are you?" asked Lisa. "Where did you come from?"

The visitor grinned in a way that made Lisa mad. "Who are you?" she repeated, and now it sounded like a command more than a question. The others laughed when Lisa turned her head away in frustration. "Okay, don't tell me. I'm going back to sleep."

The little girl with the black hair was wearing a print dress. She said in a voice that Lisa recognized, "Don't you know me?" Lisa turned her head back to look again. She squinted through the candlelight for a closer look.

Then she laughed. "Todd!" She had to admit that the disguise was good. She never did ask Jill how she'd managed to get him to dress like a girl, and she resisted the urge to tease her little brother.

After dinner Lisa briefed Todd for his mission. "Take the car. Park it in Jill's old garage. Slip into Glenbard through the tunnel and wait in the furnace room until you can hear noises upstairs. That will mean it's daytime. Then sneak into the south basement section of apartments. Be careful! Make sure that there are crowds of kids in the hallway before you walk around. Look for the Johansen family's room. They're the newest, and no one will notice if there are five Johansens instead of four. Call yourself Sherry Johansen if anyone stops you. But tell the Johansens who you really are and that their lives depend on keeping your secret. Explain it only to them. Stay with them all day until you're sure you can trust them."

Lisa stopped to think a moment and then continued. "During the day, find out two things. First, where is Logan's room? Second, what kind of defenses do they have? There's one other important thing, Todd. If it's safe . . . *if it's safe,* try to see Charlie and tell him that we're okay and that we plan to take over on May 26th—that's six days from today. And tell him that we need at least 10 cars, three large trucks, drivers to go with them, and all the guns he can sneak out.

"Tell Charlie that he shouldn't talk to anyone or do anything for two days. He has to come up with a plan of his own for getting the drivers, trucks, and guns. When he's sure it will work, he can get started. He and his team should sneak out of Glenbard on the night of May 23rd and come to the Arco station at Swift Road and North Avenue. We'll meet them there at midnight.

"If it's safe for us to show ourselves, he should flash a light across North Avenue once every minute for 12 minutes, starting at midnight. Set your watch and give it to him. Then tomorrow night, after everyone is asleep, you slip out of the Johansens' room, down the hall, and out the tunnel. But be careful—they may have guards. Here's a pistol. Keep it under your dress, and use it if you have to . . . will you?"

It's much too complicated for him, she thought. So she explained it over and over and over again, until he could repeat the mission plan without error.

"I've got it now, Lisa," he said, finally, and he went out the door and disappeared into the night.

They all worried about him. It was a dangerous mission. But he was a brave kid.

■

The next day was a nervous day for all of them. "How is Todd? How is he doing?" they asked themselves, over and over.

Craig spent most of his time outside in the warm May sunlight. Why is he out there all the time? Lisa wondered.

Her strength was slowly returning. Jill told her she'd have to rest in bed for at least a few more days. Lisa didn't like that. She had many things to do to prepare for the 23rd. But she spent the rest of the day just making plans.

Late on the first day of Todd's mission, Lisa called for Craig. "What's the matter with you?" she asked. "You're outside all the time. Don't you want to help me make plans?"

"That's funny, Lisa," he said. "It was *your* city. Your very *own* city when you owned it. Now that we have to fight to get it back, it's suddenly become *our* city."

He was right, and she knew it. Still, he hadn't answered her question. "I'm sorry," she said. "Will you help me plan the recapture of *my* city where *you'll* be safe?"

That didn't sound right either. "Craig, I didn't mean that the way it sounded. I *need* your help now, I truly do. I can't force you, I know that, and I would never want to. But will you help me?"

"No," he said flatly. "Lisa, I think you should give it up and stay here with Erika and me on this farm. Why keep fighting?"

"Give it up? Stay on this farm?"

"Lisa, we're safe here, and we can live a peaceful life. We don't have to fight anyone. We can raise our own food and let all the gangs kill each other off. I'm tired of militias and armies and spy missions. We're staying here!"

"You think you're safe here? Just about the time you've hauled in your first crops, the armies of Chidester, Elm, and Lenox will stroll right in to reap *your* harvest. What will you eat when they've taken it all away from you? Who will defend you? Erika with a pistol?"

This time, Craig challenged her. "Remember back on Grand Avenue when you said that the militia would end all our problems? You said the same thing at Glenbard, and look what's happened. What you do, Lisa, is build valuable things that everybody wants to take away from you. So far they've done it every time.

"Let them have it, Lisa. You can't fight them forever. You'll work to build Glenbard into an even richer and stronger fortress, and what you'll get for your pains will be another attack—from a bigger and smarter army. Why fight it? Stay here with us, where nobody will care about our life and our corn. At least we'll be able to live in peace.

"We're staying here," he said. "I've decided that for sure!"

"I'm sorry, Craig. I'm sorry to lose your help. Sure, I've made mistakes, I don't deny that. I've had wild ideas, and many of them have failed. Right now I'm the biggest failure in the whole world. But that's not going to stop me. I *know* we can accomplish all those things I used to talk about. We can get everything to work again, someday. But, to do it, we've got to realize that the reason for all the fighting is fear!

"What do you think makes Logan do what he does? It's fear. What do you think is the mistake almost everybody makes? They're afraid of the problem of survival. They fight and do all kinds of stupid things because they're afraid. No, I'm not giving up. It's too important. Someday you'll see it too." She turned away from her friend.

CHAPTER FIFTEEN

Well, Lisa thought, I'll just have to do it alone. But why doesn't anyone else see how simple it is?

Jill had been listening to Craig and Lisa argue. Although Lisa couldn't be sure, she guessed that Jill had taken her side.

"Jill," she said, "I think you should go back to Glenbard tomorrow. Katy and Missy must really be afraid without you. You can help Charlie with the planning . . . very secretly, of course."

Then she told Jill about her plans. Jill could help by signaling Lisa on the day of the attack.

"Logan will wonder why you've suddenly come back to the city. Tell him that I was only wounded that night. You tried to save my life, but I died. Tell him that we talked and that I didn't blame him for the shooting. I knew it was just an accident. And tell him you want to live there in Glenbard, to be with Katy and Missy, and to run the hospital. I think he'll believe you and let you stay."

It must have been two in the morning when Todd returned to the farmhouse. He told them the news in a rush of words.

Logan was having trouble running the city. He couldn't convince the citizens that Lisa was safe as his hostage. Most of the children believed the rumors that she was dead. They blamed Logan for her death and were doing everything they could to make his life miserable. He sat up late at night in the lonely chamber, trying to figure out what to do next.

Ah, Lisa thought. He's learning what it's like to sit alone in that chamber and run a city. But it must be hundreds of times harder for him than it was for me, because the citizens are against him.

Todd went on. "He treats the children cruelly. He beats the ones who give him trouble. But no one has asked, yet, about any secret entrances to the city. He beat Charlie last night and tried to get him to tell about the Secret Place, but Charlie wouldn't tell. He wouldn't tell no matter what Logan did!"

"Good for Charlie," Lisa said. "There's at least one other person who's not afraid. Good work, Todd! I know you haven't had any sleep, but can you slip back in tonight?"

"I'm not tired, Lisa. What do you want me to do?"

"Go back to the Johansens' room, sleep there, and wake up tomorrow with them. Tell Charlie that Jill will be coming in during the day. He shouldn't believe what she says. She'll tell them I'm dead. We hope Logan will be less suspicious once he learns that and won't notice Charlie sneaking out on the 23rd. Then ask Charlie to explain his plan to you so we know what's going on before we meet him at midnight."

Todd understood. In the darkness, he set off on his new mission. For the next 48 hours he would get no sleep.

Lisa was still laying on the couch, but she felt much better. She was finding new strength and new confidence. Defeat had made her think more clearly. Each problem that came up was something exciting and new to figure out.

The old warning, "take no chances," ran through her mind. *Take no chances . . . take no chances . . . look at all the possibilities . . . mistakes are costly . . . be logical . . . keep your mind clear . . . think . . . think . . . plan . . . be logical . . . take no chances!*

The words repeated themselves over and over again as she plotted the new strategy. Lisa had learned the price of carelessness.

The Great King was right, she suddenly realized. When he said that the real fun in life is earning values, he was talking about the *most* important things in life, like knowledge and love and happiness. Not just the things you can touch, like money and cars and stuff.

Just look at me, she said to herself. I've lost my city and all its treasures. But the city was only the symbol of what I had. This hasn't crushed me. Only my body was hurt. My mind is clear. My friends are still friends. And my dreams, my plans, are not impossible. They become more real each day.

What *have* I lost, really? I've made a mistake, and I'll never make it again. I've learned so much. I'm stronger than ever now. And when I get the city back . . . this time I'll be able to keep it.

She stopped suddenly, feeling self-conscious. She couldn't believe that she had found a truth. She was not quite 12 years old—it must be a dream. She shook herself, took a deep breath, got up and walked around the room.

She reviewed the list of problems that she had faced since the plague. Some of them had led to defeat, but many had ended in victory. For more than a year, she had been in constant motion, finding supplies, planning militias.

She turned back to reality. Recapturing the city wouldn't be easy, but she was ready for whatever might happen. Outside, a breeze blew against the farmhouse windows. She noticed that it would have been a good day to fly a kite.

CHAPTER SIXTEEN

The evening of May 23rd was warm and sultry. Lisa and Todd sat on their jackets and watched Swift Road for a sign of life. The Arco station was deserted, except for the dancing reflections of moon and clouds in the faces of the gas pumps.

"What time is it, Todd?"

"Five minutes to twelve."

She said nothing more until a distant rumbling was heard. "What's that? Do you think it's them?" They peered intently into the darkness.

Finally, the sounds took form. A convertible with its top down led the procession. Three soldiers accompanied a boy in the front seat. That must be Charlie, Lisa thought. The car was followed by a large dump truck with 20 soldiers in the back. Three open Jeep 4x4's and two cars were next. Each was filled with soldiers. At the end was another convertible with four more soldiers and a driver.

The convoy stopped where Swift Road met North Avenue. For a few minutes, everything was dark and silent. "What's the matter? Why isn't he signaling?" Todd asked.

Then a light flashed from the lead car. Todd and Lisa counted the seconds: ". . . 10 . . . 30 . . . 60." There was another flash of light. Then another . . .

When the signal had been repeated 12 times, Lisa and Todd walked across North Avenue and approached the first car. "Charlie, it's good to see you." She shook his hand and was in command again. "Gather all your soldiers around the Jeep in the middle. Quickly! And tell them to be quiet."

None of the soldiers, not even Charlie, knew what was planned for that night. They all wanted to cheer when they heard the voice above them on the roof of the Jeep.

"We have a long wait ahead. At daylight, we'll start a tour. It will be our first trip away from Glen Ellyn. We'll visit other cities in search of an army. When we find one that we think we can trust, then we'll make a deal with them to help us recapture Glenbard.

"We'll go to Lombard first, then to Villa Park, and then to Wheaton. If we can't find what we want, we'll try other cities. But . . . .

"You there," she said impatiently to a restless soldier. "Did you hear what I said?" He didn't answer. "Pay attention to what I'm saying. We can't take any chances tomorrow.

Who knows what we'll find in those other towns? There might be armies that will try to kill us on the spot. We must be ready, and we can't make any mistakes, so pay attention."

The soldiers rested for a time, while Lisa and Charlie sat by the gas pumps discussing the plan. When they agreed on a better way to do something, they would rouse the soldiers for more briefings. Lisa carried the plan beyond the events of the next day. Her strategy brought them to the morning of May 26th, when Charlie's soldiers and a hired army of thousands would recapture the city.

The general criticized her. "Lisa, why get ahead of ourselves? Let's take the plan one day at a time."

"No, Charlie. We have to plan the whole strategy to make sure that everything fits together. Then we can adjust it each day, as we need to, until the 26th."

They spent the whole night talking it through. The soldiers slept, were awakened, and then slept again. By morning, the plan was fixed in everyone's mind.

The eight vehicles and the army of 55 were ready. At dawn, the motorcade began the journey to Lombard. The children were tired and some were frightened by what they might discover in the "outside" world. But they all kept to their assigned positions in the vehicles.

The kids in the towns they passed were amazed by the long motorcade. Fearing that the brigade had come to do them harm, they ran into their houses. No one in these cities had yet learned to drive. The sight of one moving automobile would have surprised them, but to see eight cars and trucks filled with armed soldiers made them shudder with fear.

The motorcade stopped many times in Lombard. Lisa and Charlie tried to learn who the town leaders were. A few of the less fearful children stayed outside to watch the procession. Charlie would call out to them, "We've come in peace. Who is your leader? Where is your headquarters?"

They stopped at least 20 times, but no one would answer Charlie's questions. Lisa and Charlie decided that there was no army in Lombard. The town was dirty and lifeless.

The motorcade moved on to Villa Park. What they saw there was something that no one wanted to speak of. It was a town that hadn't survived. Death was everywhere. The children felt its presence on every street of the town, and they didn't need to look inside a single house to know what they would find inside. They drove away silently.

In Wheaton they found a leader, a headquarters, *and* an army, but not the alliance they were looking for. The general of Wheaton was a cruel, violent boy. "Get your army out of here," he said. "Or my men will wipe you out. My name is Scott Donald Mennie, and I have 200 soldiers."

"Scott Donald Mennie?" a voice called from the ranks. "You look more to me like Scott Donald Duck!" The small army of Glenbard laughed, and Lisa studied the angry general. He was shaking.

He chose to ignore the insult. "You'll be smart if you just stay in your own town and don't stick your necks out of it again—ever!" Then he told them why. "I'm going to join with the Chicago army, and we'll be seeing you someday soon. So don't try anything clever, or you'll just give us a good reason to wipe you out right now."

Then he started to brag. "The Chicago army is huge. It has more than 2,000 soldiers. When Wheaton and other towns join up, it'll have even more. Maybe as many as 5,000 by this summer. When we're ready, we'll start to capture towns like yours one at a time, until we control the whole state."

He talks too much, Lisa thought.

But he wasn't finished yet. "If you're smart, you'll join us. If you're not smart, you'll regret it. The King of Chicago is powerful. He'll make you a good offer. You'll have a chance, and you better take advantage of it. Now get out of here!"

Suddenly he held up his hand. "But wait. What's your leader's name? Is he here? I want to give his name to the king."

When Lisa stepped forward, the boy laughed. "It can't be!" He laughed again, and this time he looked at the 55 soldiers. "A girl!" he mocked. "What's the matter with you guys? You must be some tough army! "

Lisa had never wanted to hurt anyone, not even Tom Logan. But now she smashed her fist into the face of the Wheaton general.

He reeled backward but stayed on his feet. The blood from his nose confused him long enough for the motorcade to pull away. A girl! he thought, as he stared after them in amazement.

"Well," said Charlie to Lisa, "We've got another enemy now . . . Scott Donald Duck!" They roared with laughter. Suddenly serious again, Charlie added, "That Chicago army stuff scares me. What do you think of it, Lisa?"

"The King of Chicago," she said. "What a dumb name for a leader. Why not president or premier? Is this the Dark Ages or something?"

Neither of them answered. They both knew that it *was* like the Dark Ages. Kings and brutality and plagues and death were again a part of life. And Lisa knew that Logan was only her first enemy, not her last. If she recaptured Glenbard, she would be facing even bigger armies in the future. The Dark Ages wouldn't end for a long time.

"Where to now, Lisa?" Charlie asked.

"Well, we *could* look at other towns. But I really don't think we'll find anything much different. We're going to have to revise our plan tonight. We'll just have to do it without a big army." Lisa thought a while.

"Driver," she said, "turn here. Left." Lisa led the motorcade safely back to the farm on Swift Road.

But it wasn't the quiet farm that they had expected to find. The high flames and smoke in the farmyard reminded Lisa of her burning house. The loud voices made her think of past battles and celebrations.

Which was it? she wondered as the motorcade came to rest in front of the farm. Was it a party, or was it trouble?

It was definitely a party—there were shouts and

cheers of joy as she walked toward the crowd in the farmyard. They had been singing the Glenbard song and waiting for the return of the motorcade. The orange-and-yellow flag of Glenbard was flying high above the bonfire. Yes, they were celebrating.

Someone had learned that Lisa was alive and staying at a farm on Swift Road. The rumor had spread quickly through the city, and this group must have sneaked out after Charlie.

"Charlie!" Lisa was angry now. "How could this happen? How did they find out? Don't you realize what could happen? This could be our *big* mistake. Logan might come here after us. Even if he doesn't, now he'll be on guard every minute against an attack. Tell me, Charlie! How could they have found out? Only you and Todd knew about it."

Charlie couldn't say anything. He stood there with his mouth open, thinking. Finally he said, "Lisa, I swear I didn't tell a soul. I swear it. I can't imagine how they found out. I didn't even say we were going to the Arco station."

She believed him. And then she remembered Jill. They must have tortured her, she thought.

The crowd wanted Lisa to speak to them. They cheered and shouted, "We want Lisa! We want Lisa!" But her mind was on other things, very serious things. Would Logan come tonight? What had happened to Jill? Was she hurt? What should they do next? Could they still attack on the 26th? Could this bunch in the farmyard serve as an army?

All through the night the crowd grew louder. They kept shouting, "Lisa! Lisa! We want Lisa!"

But she didn't speak to them. Instead, she sat alone in a room inside the farmhouse and replanned the strategy. The words of caution came back to haunt her . . . *take no chances . . . look at all the possibilities . . . mistakes are costly . . . think . . . plan . . . be logical . . . take no chances . . .*

Outside, the noise continued. No, she couldn't speak to them yet. When her plan was ready, she would talk. After all, you should only speak when you have something to say.

Mysteriously, the crowd was growing larger by the hour. How was it possible? Where did they all come from—those 200, and then 300? What had happened at the city?

The answer, if she'd had time to look for it, could have been seen on Swift Road, across North Avenue, down the old route to Grand Avenue, and, finally, past the lake to the castle itself. The roads were filled with a stream of pilgrims carrying their life's belongings and food and guns to find a leader who had come back from the dead.

But in the darkness of her room, Lisa's courage wavered. I'm not what they think, she said to herself. I don't know if we can do it. I just don't know.

The moment of weakness left her as she turned her thoughts to the problem, the one she *knew* she could solve. Enough doubting, she warned herself. I've got to make this plan right—perfect—no chances—no mistakes . . .

All that night and the next day Lisa kept to herself in the room. Is this the 25th? she wondered. Tonight—by tonight I *must* have the plan ready.

The crowd of 300 waited patiently outside in the warm spring air. They never doubted that everything would be all right and that she would figure something out.

Todd came to work by her side. Together, by candlelight, they looked at plans and drawings. To those waiting outside, it seemed they would never come out.

"What are they doing in there?" the children asked. "Why won't she come out here? Why can't we go get Logan?"

Charlie assured them. "It's an important plan, a very important plan. We can't make any mistakes, and we can't take any chances! You have to trust her. She knows what to do."

And when Lisa was ready—when she told them the new plan—it went into effect immediately.

In what seemed to be almost the next moment, the crowd was at the castle. They took positions in the woods and by the walls and in the trees around Glenbard. No one made a sound while Lisa crept through the secret tunnel alone.

Would he be in the chamber? Was her gun loaded? Did she have the key ready? Would there be guards?

What was wrong? She emerged from the tunnel inside the fortress. But there were no guards anywhere! No children anywhere . . . what was the matter? She was more nervous than she would have been had they been everywhere.

She went through the basement. There were no guards, no citizens. Up the stairs to the main floor—nothing, not a soul anywhere. She went down the corridor. It was deserted, lifeless. She found her way to the old chamber and turned the key.

Logan was sitting there as though he had been waiting. "Hello, Lisa" he said, and then added, "Sit down. I want to talk to you."

She hadn't expected this.

"I can't handle your city, Lisa. You win. Your citizens rebelled and just walked out. How could I stop them? What could I do?

"Lisa, I'm sorry for the shooting, really sorry. I told them not to shoot. It was an accident. I didn't want you to get hurt. And your friend, Jill, they'll tell you that I hurt her, too. But I didn't. We just scared her a little. She's safe in a room downstairs. We just scared her, Lisa, that's all. Your citizens found out where you were—I think she told them—and I threatened to hurt her if the others left, but they were too busy running away to hear me. They just walked out. What else could I do? They hated me from the start. What could I do?"

Is he asking my opinion? she wondered. Logan seemed spent and weary. He had faced the problems of the city, and he didn't care any longer. He was beaten.

"Okay, let's talk," Lisa said, and she laid the gun on the table beside the candle.

It was a trick. In an instant, he grabbed the gun, aimed it at her, and shouted a signal to 50 hidden guards, who soon filled the hall outside. For the second time in the history of Glenbard, the gang leader was smiling victoriously at her.

CHAPTER SEVENTEEN

The door closed. Lisa and Tom were alone in the tower chamber. She forgot about the danger for a moment and thought about the many hours she had passed in front of the candle in this dark room. She had spent entire nights planning for the future and worrying and hoping. Now she was back, but the room didn't belong to her. Why should it? she wondered. How could I fall for such a simple trick? She didn't deserve the room or the city.

"Why does it have to be this way, Tom?" she said, not knowing where the conversation would lead. "Why do we have to fight? You know I don't want to fight. Have I ever attacked you before? This time I'm only defending what's mine!

"What is it about you that makes you want to fight and steal? Are you afraid that you can't earn things for yourself? Why do you need to steal what others have worked for?"

Tom listened, but he couldn't reply. She had found his weakness and that was painful.

Lisa went on. "What good is your life, Tom? Did you ever wonder about that? What fun is there in your kind of dirty business? What good is there in making people afraid of you? Why do you need slaves or soldiers who are afraid of you? You depend on fear!

"You start with your soldiers' fear of death and starvation, and then you add to that your own fear of failure. I think you fear building a better life with your own brains.

"You know, Tom, that's what it is. You don't have the guts to depend on your own resources. No! You'd rather be tough and take what someone else has worked hard for.

"Do you have any idea what this city cost me, Tom? I paid for this place with hard work. I didn't steal anything that belonged to anyone else. I just used my head.

"And then you . . . you came along with your army and your guns and decided that my work was ripe for the harvest."

Tom had no answer. He put the gun down on the table and slumped into his chair. He couldn't think of a reply or a boast or a threat. He was silent.

Lisa watched the gun but didn't pick it up. She had a much better weapon now—his fear. She had Tom Logan against the wall. He had no more defenses. She would drive home the final blow.

"You're afraid of life and your ability to earn your way through it. I feel sorry for you. You don't know what real fun is." She wanted to give him the Great King's happiness advice. But Logan wasn't ready for it. She picked up the gun and pointed it at him, her finger on the trigger. Then she made a decision. She put the weapon back down.

"You're free, Tom," she said. "Go away, and take your army with you."

He said nothing and moved to the door. She added, "I'd like to be able to like you, Tom."

Within minutes, the Chidester, Elm, and Lenox army was walking away from Glenbard. Lisa closed the chamber door. Her gun was sitting on the table near her old familiar candle.

"Alone!" she said out loud. It felt good to be back. She wandered around the room, deep in thought, while her city filled with happy citizens. The hall was crowded, and they were waiting to see her.

There was a knock at the chamber door. It was Todd. "Well, we're back, aren't we, Todd?" She smiled at him.

"They want you to speak to them, Lisa."

"What? About what? There are hundreds of them out there. Let me rest a minute. You should go to sleep, Todd, over there, on the couch. I'll tell you a story tomorrow. Will that be all right?

"You must be tired," she said. "You haven't slept in days, have you? I'm tired too. Maybe one day soon we can take a vacation somehow, somewhere."

Lisa gazed at her brave little brother. He had already fallen asleep.

After a time, the noise from the hall distracted her.

What do they want? she wondered. Why do they waste their time shouting for me? Why don't they spend the effort on something else?

She sat back down and lit the candle. It was her "thoughtful" candle. Its flame had inspired the plans that had made her city.

The shouts from the hall became insistent. "We want Lisa! We want Lisa!" It sounded as though all the citizens were there, waiting and chanting.

She wanted to please them. But she didn't know what to say. Should she tell them about the Great King, or the "King of Chicago"? Should she mention the army of 5,000 that might attack their city?

She had to speak to them. It was her job. She paused by the door, not wanting to make her appearance and not wanting to spoil her hard-earned peace.

Lisa stood for a long time with her hand on the door latch. I don't know how, she thought, but I'll figure out a way to show them what I know. We have to make plans. We have to prepare.

The girl who owned the city walked through the door into the waiting crowd of happy children.

ABOUT THE AUTHOR

O. T. Nelson's initial impetus for writing a novel was to help pay for an expansion of his house-painting business, but his work has gone on to become much more than that to generations of readers. *The Girl Who Owned a City* was first published in 1975 and has been popular ever since. O. T. Nelson explains that he wanted children "to realize that they are important and that they have the ability to think and make a difference." His own life is reflected in the story. He wrote the book while living in the Chicago suburb of Glen Ellyn, Illinois— the setting of the story—and the novel's protagonists, Lisa and Todd Nelson, share the names of his own children. O. T. Nelson lives in Minnesota with his wife.

THE GIRL WHO OWNED A CITY

O. T. NELSON DAN JOLLEY JOËLLE JONES JENN MANLEY LEE